JUDGE RANDALL
HAS DOUBTS

JUDGE RANDALL
HAS DOUBTS

TONY ROGERS

A Judge Randall Mystery

ISBN: 978-1-7356835-2-2 (Paperback)
ISBN: 978-1-7356835-3-9 (Ebook)

Published by Quinn Cove Books

Cover Design by Berge Design

To my sister, Dale Rogers Marshall
1937-2021

1

"Judge Randall?"

Jim looked up. "Yes?"

The woman appeared to be in her late forties. "May I sit down?"

"Who are you?"

"My name is Deborah Ryan. You convicted my husband of murder twenty years ago."

"Max Ryan. I remember. Please, sit down."

She took her handbag off her shoulder and placed it on an empty chair. The Long Gone was half full that morning, the wake-up crowd having left, the lunch contingent having yet to arrive. Jim's favorite time at the coffee house.

"You remember."

"A judge doesn't forget his first murder trial."

"Max is coming up for parole next month, Judge. His second try. His first try failed because he refused to admit guilt. I'm afraid he'll be turned down again because he still denies he was the killer."

"It's none of my business, Mrs. Ryan."

"Have you ever had doubts about the case, sir?"

"I have doubts about almost everything. About your husband's case in particular? No, I haven't."

"Max is no saint. I'm not saying he is, but I know Max. He's not a killer."

"A jury said he is. I'm sorry, Mrs. Ryan."

"Max has never lost hope. You ought to see him, Judge Randall. Prison's taken a toll on him physically, but not mentally. He's an inspiration."

"He sounds impressive. I wish the two of you luck at his parole hearing."

"Could you speak up for him, Judge? Could you do that?"

"That's rarely if ever done, Mrs. Ryan, even if I were inclined to do so."

"Could you at least write a letter? Please, Judge Randall. He doesn't stand a chance without you if he won't admit he's guilty and say he's sorry."

"I'm afraid not. Now if you'll excuse me."

She stood but didn't leave, and he got a good look at her, haggard but not broken. A woman who had lived with a burden for so long she had become defined by it. A woman beyond bitterness, clinging to a slender hope.

"Thank you for your time," she said.

"Before you go, how did you know you could find me here?"

"Your habits are legendary at the courthouse. They say routine is everything to you." A smile creased her lips ever so slightly. "Take care."

She left. A moment later she reappeared and retrieved her handbag from the empty chair. "I do that all the time," she gave an embarrassed shrug and departed.

The Long Gone had windows but you wouldn't know it, judging by the meager amount of light that forced its way in. What was it about America and dark places? In America, coffee houses like The Long Gone were places to hide, not people watch or be seen.

He remembered Max Ryan's case. In general, he remembered details of murder trials better than details of his own personal life, and he especially remembered the Ryan case because it was his first. A hedge fund manager named Spinner had died of arsenic poisoning after eating dinner at the Fish and Fowl, where Max Ryan was the assistant pastry chef. The murder was traced to a Meyer lemon semifreddo, Spinner's favorite dessert, which Ryan prepared for Spinner whenever he ate at the restaurant. Spinner insisted that Max Ryan and only Max Ryan prepare the semifreddo, said that no one else made it like Ryan did, and Spinner was a frequent enough customer that the restaurant complied. At the time Jim thought it unfair that only Max Ryan was on trial when no one, including the DA, thought the murder was his idea, but Ryan steadfastly refused to reveal the name of the person who put him up to it even though the DA had been ready to plea bargain. I didn't poison Spinner, he said over and over; how can I give up someone who doesn't exist? The man or woman who wanted Spinner dead was never identified. Jim felt that Max Ryan was the designated fall guy but by the end of the trial had no doubts of his complicity.

Jim sat for a long time thinking about Deborah Ryan's words. The longer he sat, the more disturbed he became. Deeply disturbed. Why? Old cases usually didn't haunt him.

He skipped lunch and made himself soup and a sandwich for dinner. Pat came over after dinner.

"What did you eat?" she asked.

"I don't remember."

"Are you okay?"

They sat at the kitchen table and he told her of Deborah Ryan appearing at The Long Gone, what she said and how it disturbed him. "I don't know why. I heard many murder cases after Ryan's."

"Maybe because this was your first."

"That, and I'm also troubled by the fact that Max Ryan was willing to remain in prison rather than admit he killed Michael Spinner. We both know that the majority of candidates for parole will say how sorry they are for their crime and talk about how they turned their lives around while in prison in hopes of release. Denial of guilt is rare."

"Are you going to follow up?"

"Never. I'm going to put it behind me, where it was before Mrs. Ryan appeared and where it belongs. What?" Pat had given him a skeptical look. "You don't believe me?"

"I never doubt your sincerity."

"I mean it, Pat. I've been off the bench for over two years."

"That hasn't stopped you so far."

"Hasn't stopped me from getting involved in solving crimes. The crime in this case occurred over twenty years ago, and a man has served time for it. Case closed."

Jim's retirement from the bench had been anything but tranquil. He had helped a young man escape charges of vehicular homicide and solved the murder of a hate spewing preacher caught between two dueling religious cults. He wasn't complaining. Better than boredom, yet he was tired. Boredom beckoned.

But there was no harm in talking to Ted Conover about the Ryan case. He had known Ted for over twenty years since both were newly appointed officers of the court:

Ted Conover a very junior assistant district attorney, Jim a very green judge of the Massachusetts Superior Court, the trial court for the Commonwealth of Massachusetts. They hadn't known each other well then. Only when Jim had become an established jurist and Ted had become the long-standing number two in the DA's office did they become friends, but even then their respective roles kept them from becoming close. That had changed with Jim's retirement. Since Jim's retirement, Ted had become an invaluable ally.

Jim was a do-gooder with a scowl and a quip; Ted a workhorse who mostly played it straight but wasn't above a feint or two to distract a judge or a defense attorney. Fierce in legal battles, trustworthy in personal matters, a loyal friend: Ted Conover.

Jim texted Ted: "Got time to meet?"

Ted's office wasn't far from the Middlesex County Courthouse, where Jim had been a judge. The office was bare-bones, pictures of Ted's wife and children on the desk the only decoration. Sitting behind his desk, Ted looked diminished, standing he looked impressive. He stood to shake Jim's hand.

"How's the family?" Jim asked as he sat down.

"My wife and daughter are into horses in a big way, can you imagine? I expect to find hay bales in the dining room any day. How's Pat?"

"Doing well. Her memoir *Bench Life* is coming along nicely. Her publisher expects big things."

"Good for her. I hope she said nice things about me."

"She says terrible things about you, all of which you deserve. Think back, Ted, think back to when you were eager and handsome."

"You mean last week?"

"Twenty-one years ago, the trial of Max Ryan, convicted of second-degree murder in the death of Michael Spinner. You were a rookie ADA, I was a brand new judge. I freely admit being so green that I spent more time worrying what trial procedures I had messed up than whether the outcome was just."

"You have doubts now?"

"I have curiosity. He's up for parole soon, and the mastermind behind the killing has never been found. Can you pull your case file and tell me if you notice anything unusual?"

"You're not planning to get involved, are you? You would never do a foolhardy thing like that, would you?"

"His wife wants me to. But I'm not planning anything. Satisfying my curiosity, that's all."

"You mean like you satisfied your curiosity when you came to Ernie Farrell's arraignment?"

"You set me up for that. And look where it's gotten me, in your office, a supplicant once more. Will you help me?"

"You know I will."

Jim walked back to Pat's via the Longfellow Bridge. He liked the expansive view better than the scrunched-up view from the science museum aqueduct. As he reached the bridge's apogee, a Red Line train rumbled past, its antiquated cars looking like relics from a history museum. The bridge was in terrible shape, but at least repairs to the bridge were scheduled. The view, by contrast, mesmerized, the broad Charles River basin dotted with sailboats and whitecaps. Nature does not defer maintenance.

By the time Jim reached the end of the bridge, the idea of getting involved in an old case like Michael Spinner's death seemed nonsensical. Pat's apartment was nearby and he felt safe and settled when he was with her. They kept separate dwellings but spent the majority of their evenings together. A long marriage that left him a widower, a solid relationship with Pat, no dependents to worry about, a successful career behind him – he had a good life. Why stir things up again when he had it so good?

2

If he had to pick Pat's place or his as a place to spend the rest of his life, Jim would probably pick Pat's Beacon Hill apartment. He liked hills in general (to wit, his house on a hill in Vermont), and Beacon Hill's labyrinth of streets was charming. He liked her apartment: bowfront windows in the living room, compact but well-equipped kitchen, two bedrooms, one of which doubled as Pat's office and a guest room. Most importantly the apartment came with Pat, a steely ex-judge capable of an imperious gaze when dealing with bone-headed attorneys, but genuine, witty, and wry off the bench. Since they had become a couple, Jim had known a peace he hadn't known before, not even with Joyce, his late wife. Peace and no bullshit. Pat.

Pat was in her office emailing her editor while Jim lounged on the living room sofa, laptop on his knees, seeing what he could find online about Max Ryan. Not much, it turned out, the case having been tried in the pre-digital age. His mind did one of its zigzags, and he wondered if future TV watchers will draw a blank when they watch a pre-digital police procedural with detectives frantically yanking paper folders out of metal file cabinets.

He did find articles about the case. It turned out that the *Boston Globe* had covered the story in more than the usual depth since the story had everything a newspaper could want – hedge fund wealth, trendy restaurant, poison. Money, food, murder. Hot stuff.

Max Ryan had grown up on the streets of South Boston, raised by a single mom who supported four kids by herself after her husband took off, never to be heard from again. She attended evening classes at a community college while working in an elementary school cafeteria, and after earning her associate's degree got a job as a lab tech at University Hospital. Colleagues of hers were quoted as saying she was a tireless worker, never acted sorry about her lot in life, and was quietly proud her kids had mostly stayed out of trouble. After Max's arrest, she never wavered in her belief that he was innocent. She died while Max was in prison; he was not allowed out to attend her funeral.

Max grew up knowing the life of the streets, yet he somehow avoided the worst of it, never joining a gang nor antagonizing one (a neat trick if you could pull it off). Minor offenses (breaking a school window, a street scuffle or two) but nothing major. He was rough-hewn but soft-hearted, the kind of person who could absorb the troubles of others without becoming a troublemaker. He loved food from a young age, according to his mother, but never expressed an interest in the food business until he got a summer job as a dishwasher at a neighborhood dive bar. After he graduated high school, he landed a job at La Cote Bretonnerie pouring water and folding napkins of patrons who had left their tables to use the restrooms, and at the time of his arrest, he was assistant pastry chef at Fish and Fowl, the financial district's restaurant du jour for the newly-moneyed.

Pat entered the living room, waving the revised galleys of her memoir. "Want to see?"

Jim, distracted by Max Ryan's story, leafed through them. "Very nice," he said, handing them back.

Pat smiled. "Such enthusiasm. Jealous? Keep in mind...."

Jim interrupted her. "If I had done my share, etcetera, etcetera."

"Well? Isn't it true?"

"Yes, but that doesn't mean you need to constantly remind me."

"Why not? It's fun." She sat down beside him. "What have you learned about Max Ryan?"

"Doesn't seem like the kind of young man who would be involved in murder. He had plenty of opportunities to go wrong in his teens, but avoided them all."

She kissed Jim on the cheek. "I knew you couldn't resist getting involved."

"Stop it," he said.

"Why?" She smiled.

"How can I concentrate?"

She kissed him again.

"You're just doing that to distract me," he said. "Stop."

She rose. "You don't deserve me. Want to go out for lunch?"

A pub at the base of the hill served lunch. They never ate there because it was truly a dive, but Jim insisted on eating there this day. "Max Ryan once worked in a dive. I used to drink in dives when I was young. I want to refresh my memory."

"You were young once?"

"Stop it. You're annoying me."

They entered the pub, dark at noon. Jim had frequented dives in law school, but it had been a long time and he had forgotten the rancid smell of stale beer and urine that was universal in dives. Did it come in spray cans? Were dogs invited to pee in corners?

Even Pat was taken aback. "Are you sure you want to chance the food here, you who are deathly afraid of food poisoning?"

"Maybe not. Let's have a drink, then leave."

"Or forget the drink and leave now."

"I came here for a purpose. Don't thwart me. Did I get in the way of your memoir?"

"No. Nor did you help me with *our* memoir."

"What's on tap?" Jim said to the barman.

"Bud and Bud Light."

"Nothing local?"

"Budweiser's made in New Hampshire."

"I'll have a glass of red wine." Jim turned to Pat. "Imagine being a teenager washing dishes in a place like this. I did all kinds of summer jobs when I was young, but I have a hard time imagining myself smelling this smell and seeing this enervating light every day and entering the food business anyway. Max Ryan must have had a calling for food, not to be turned off by washing dishes in a dive like this."

Jim's phone rang. He extracted it from his pocket, always a challenge. "Hello?"

"Jim, it's Ted. I pulled our file on the Max Ryan case. Here's a capsule version of the salient facts. The day after Michael Spinner died, an anonymous caller to our office reported hearing Max Ryan threaten Michael Spinner the night he died."

"Male caller? Female caller?"

"Male. Said he worked at the Fish and Fowl. Hung up when we asked for his name. We never found evidence of threats, but soon after the call, traces of arsenic were found on Max Ryan's clothing. When we interviewed the kitchen staff, a newly hired line cook recalled seeing Ryan sprinkle a powdery substance on Michael Spinner's semifreddo just before it was carried to the dining room. So Max Ryan quickly became the prime suspect. You know the rest because you heard the case."

"Thanks, Ted. If you remember anything else, let me know." Jim's wine arrived. He took a sip. "Good god!"

"Your nose just did a back flip," Pat said.

"I can't drink this. Let's get out of here."

Jim tossed some money on the bar, and they walked out into daylight that seemed painfully bright by comparison.

"What did Ted say?"

"That an anonymous caller reported hearing Max Ryan threaten Michael Spinner. That's not consistent with what I know about the young Max Ryan. I have to learn more about Ryan, but how? Help me."

"How?"

"I don't know."

"That narrows it down."

"One thing I won't do is talk to Ryan's wife again."

"You definitely don't want to talk to her. That would be the worst way to learn about Max Ryan."

"I don't want to raise her hopes that I'll help her husband."

Pat didn't reply.

Jim waited. "By your silence you're saying that I'm going to help, and that I'll talk to her eventually."

"Something like that."

"Don't be smug. The law of averages says you'll be right once in a while."

She smiled, primly.

*

As an ad hoc sleuth, Jim did not employ an investigator, but Ernie Farrell was the nearest equivalent. Ernie's computer skills made him the perfect fact-digger in a digital age, and he owed Jim big-time; Jim had successfully defended him in a vehicular homicide case after stepping down from the bench. To a lesser degree, Jim owed Ernie, as Ernie was the one who introduced Jim to The Long Gone, which had since become Jim's hangout/meeting place of choice.

"I've got an assignment for you, if you care to accept it. My first murder trial as a judge was the case of Max Ryan, a young man then, now serving twenty-five to life for the murder of a hedge fund manager named Michael Spinner. His wife came here looking for me a few days ago and asked me to appear before the parole board on her husband's behalf."

Ernie's face had matured in the relatively short time Jim had known him. His eyes had lost their youthful insolence and now had purpose. "What can I do?" Ernie said.

"See what you can find about Max Ryan before he was arrested. What I remember is that he lived in the South End with his mother, washed dishes during the summer in high school, then got into the restaurant business and was working his way up when Michael Spinner was killed."

"Was he working his way up the food chain?" Ernie asked.

"What?" Jim said, confused. "Oh, I get it. Yes, in fact."

"Terrible joke," Ernie said. "Nerd humor."

"You're an ex-nerd, Ernie. Now you're an amateur investigator helping an old judge meddle."

"Anyone who knows a half a dozen languages of code like I do is a nerd. Once a nerd, always a nerd. Why are you interested in such an old case?"

"Talking to Ryan's wife jogged my memory. Ryan was convicted by a jury, and I agreed with the verdict. The sentence was pretty much dictated by statute. What bothered me then – still does – was that Ryan clearly was not the person who wanted Spinner dead. Somebody put him up to it. Someday who had motive to kill Spinner and the means to get Ryan to do it."

Ernie thought out loud. "Did Ryan have a drug habit?"

"Not as far as I know."

"Gambling debts?"

"Same answer."

"Or maybe the answer is the simplest one: money, someone paid Max Ryan lots and lots of money."

Jim continued Ernie's train of thought. "Someone with a grudge against Michael Spinner. See what you can find out. Do your magic."

*

Sasha Cohen was another of Jim's sources as a sleuth. A fledgling reporter for an alternative weekly when they met, Sasha now reported for the Boston *Globe* and had access to its morgue, where old stories go to die.

She agreed to meet him at a popular bar in Kenmore Square. She had a breezy manner and a relentless mind. "Haven't seen you in ages. You don't look worse for wear."

"Appearances deceive," he replied. The bar buzzed with young professionals.

Jim generally had a crush on one young woman per case: Sasha Cohen was his crush in the Watson murder. Jim's crushes generally had a short shelf-life. Sasha remained a friend and a source.

Sasha leaned slightly forward and narrowed her eyes. "Who do you want to expose and humiliate this time?"

"Michael Spinner, murdered more than twenty years ago."

She leaned back, eyes wide. "Never heard of him."

"Because you were like ten then."

"Who was he? Why are you interested?"

"A successful money man, ran a hedge fund called Fast Forward. No motive for his murder was ever determined but a young man named Max Ryan was convicted based on arsenic found on his clothing and a tip-off from a fellow employee who thought he saw Ryan sprinkle something unusual on Spinner's Meyer lemon semifreddo. Ryan was the assistant pastry chef at a restaurant where Spinner was such a good customer that Ryan had standing orders to prepare his favorite dessert for him whenever he came in. Only Ryan's Meyer lemon semifreddo passed Spinner's muster. Spinner's death and Ryan's subsequent trial were covered by the *Globe*, and I'd appreciate any background information you can dig up."

"You answered my first question, but not the second. Why are you interested?"

"I was the judge in the case. I sentenced Ryan to twenty-five years to life after a jury found him guilty. He's up for his second try at parole soon, and for reasons I can't quite fathom – maybe sheer restlessness – I have doubts about the verdict."

He reflected for a moment before he continued. "It's strange how time can distort memory, make something that seemed crystal-clear seem murky, or vice versa. Or maybe time has unearthed a clue that my mind buried so deeply I couldn't see it until now. I want to ease my conscience."

"This is what I like about you, Jim," Sasha said.

"That I'm a tortured human being?"

"Exactly."

"You're supposed to say no."

She lifted her glass. "Cheers."

3

Who was Michael Spinner? Jim sat in his leather chair with his head back, eyes closed, remembering what he could about the trial. Hedge funds were nothing new, but didn't become a hot item for wealthy investors until the '90's. As the economy boomed and the rich got richer, the richest of the rich sought novel ways to maximize their wealth, and hedge funds obliged, investing in commodity futures, real estate, and risky debt instruments the stodgy firms wouldn't touch. Hedge funds promised results and exclusivity, and as long as the economy buoyed them, they had no trouble attracting clients. The catch – from an investor's standpoint – were the fees hedge funds charged: 2 percent commission on every trade, plus 20 percent of whatever profits resulted; tolerable when markets were soaring, problematic when profits fell.

Michael Spinner had stayed out of the news before his death, and no one knew him well. The business associates who gave victim statements at Max Ryan's sentencing spoke glowingly about him – devoted husband, lover of fine wines, generous supporter of local charities, his death a great loss to the community, etc. – but Jim recalled not being moved by their pro forma recitations. He got the sense that what his associates most liked about Spinner was his ability to generate profits for the hedge fund. As a man, a human being, Michael Spinner apparently inspired little loyalty.

He heard Pat's footsteps on the stairs. A moment later, her head in the door. "Can you take a break?"

"For you, of course, but it better be good."

"Isn't it always?"

He stood and briefly embraced her.

"Were you thinking dirty thoughts?" she asked.

"I was thinking about hedge funds. So, yes, dirty thoughts. Actually it was your coming upstairs which got to me, you so rarely come to my lair."

"The height *is* intoxicating. To be serious for a moment, I need your advice."

"Sit down."

"My editor wants more about us in the book."

"Is that a problem?"

"Not with me, but you like to control your image and might not like what I say."

"You'll let me read it ahead of time, I assume. If I object, I'll say so."

"So you won't mind if I go into detail?"

"Anatomical?"

Pat laughed. "Yes, with pictures. Close-ups." She covered her eyes. "I'll never recover from that image."

Jim's mind had left the room. "Who would want to kill a hedge fund manager?"

"I knew it. I knew you'd get involved."

"Don't gloat. Answer my question, please."

"An investor who lost his or her fortune in the hedge fund."

"Next question, who do we know who might name names?"

Pat had gone to college with Beth Gordon, executive vice-president of Third Generation Investors, Inc., an investment fund for old-line families and other investors who desired gain with minimum publicity. Gordon herself came from an old-line New England family, a family of discreet wealth and quiet philanthropy.

Jim and Pat met Beth Gordon in the bar of the Charles Hotel. Gordon in person was someone you wouldn't notice in a crowd, more Little League mom than money-maven. At first, as Jim listened to the two of them catch up on old times, Gordon seemed almost hapless in manner, not at all sharp, but when Jim asked what she knew about Michael Spinner, she grew focused.

"I apparently touched a nerve," Jim said.

"His reputation in my world was mixed. There were some who attributed his success to his salesmanship, some who thought he was gifted when it came to markets, others who thought his success was all a con. To the limited extent I knew him, I didn't like him, but the way his death unleashed the bullies of the press infuriated me. From the press coverage, you'd think that Michael deserved what he got and Max Ryan was the victim. I get so tired of the stereotyping of the rich."

"I assume Pat told you that I was the judge in Max Ryan's trial."

Gordon nodded. "She did. Forgive me for venting. You conducted a fair trial in the eyes of the Street. Why are you asking about Michael Spinner at this late date?"

"Max Ryan is up for parole this year. It bothered me during his trial and still does that we never learned why he would want Spinner dead. I'm satisfying my curiosity."

"Do you second-guess all your cases?"

"No, this is unusual. Can you tell me more about Michael Spinner's hedge fund?"

Gordon thought carefully before she replied. "The clients of my fund, Third Generation Investments, are patient and discreet, more concerned about preserving family wealth than maximizing short term growth. Spinner's hedge fund was the opposite. He liked fast and splashy. His investors were the go-go types, the alpha males who often had violent tempers. I can see one of them going ballistic when Spinner's fund tanked."

"How far did it fall?"

"Rumor had it that it almost went belly-up. There was talk of the fund being little more than a Ponzi scheme."

"Did you believe that?"

"No, not personally. As I said, I barely knew Michael, but from what I knew, he was capable of gross exaggeration of his brilliance but wasn't a crook."

The bar in the Charles Hotel, a gathering place for Harvard academics, was more used to talk of Spinoza than Spinner, more accustomed to arcane disputations of minutiae than talk of Ponzi schemes. "So, what do you think?" Jim asked Pat when Beth Gordon had left the bar.

"She didn't paint a pretty picture of Michael Spinner."

"She's not alone in her opinion of him. Shall we go home?"

"Your place or mine?"

"Mine's closer."

Cambridge is at its best in the dusk, a neither here nor there time of day, the perfect time of day for a community that endlessly argues alternatives. Jim dithered like an academic when he had the luxury, but he was smugly confident of his ability to make decisions.

"Jim, are you sure you want to get even more deeply involved in this case? Old wounds, etcetera. What if you made a grievous mistake twenty years ago? Will it sully your opinion of your career?"

Jim walked a few steps before replying. "I don't think so. But there's only one way to find out."

They arrived on Jim's street. The street was quiet. Talk of sullying his career turned Jim nostalgic. "We're doing okay, aren't we? You and me," Jim asked.

"I'm not sure exactly what you mean. As a couple?"

"Yes."

"As a couple, we're doing great. Why do you ask? Is everything okay?"

"A sixty-eight year old man at dusk, that's all. Gratitude is an emotion I had almost forgotten before I met you. By the way, I like you better as a lover than as a colleague."

Which made her laugh. They entered his townhouse. He turned on the light. "Why do you laugh?"

"Because you're adorable."

"I am not. Never say that about me again. I am wise and dignified. Say that."

"You are adorable."

*

Lunch with Enrique Montgomery, the young relatively new head of the FBI's Boston office. Jim had gotten to know and like him during the Watson case. He didn't look like a G-man, he looked like a grad student – khaki pants, open shirts. His father was from Mexico, his mother from Minnesota.

They ate at a deli near government center. For the most part, Enrique put up with Jim's meddling; having a former judge looking over his shoulder was, for the most part, a good thing. "Don't tell me you're at it again," Enrique said.

"Yes, I am. Want to make something of it?"

"Not unless you make me look bad. What case are you meddling in this time?"

"A case I heard over twenty years ago. A man named Max Ryan has been serving time for murder and is up for parole."

"Who was the victim?"

"A hedge fund manager named Michael Spinner. Ryan was an assistant pastry chef at the restaurant where Spinner ate shortly before he died of arsenic poisoning. Ryan prepared the same dessert for Spinner every time he ate at the Fish and Fowl. Eyewitness testimony from another kitchen worker and arsenic traces on Ryan's clothes convinced the jury of his guilt. In hindsight, the evidence was borderline, but at the time the jury had no trouble reaching a verdict, and I had no qualms about sentencing him."

"But you have qualms now?"

"Not qualms. Questions."

"Have you ever thought of taking up a hobby, vintage cars perhaps or skeet shooting. Anything to keep you busy."

"Face it, I am a great asset to law enforcement."

Enrique managed to keep a straight face. "You want to know what I know about the case, right?"

"About the case, and about Max Ryan and Michael Spinner."

"Way before my time, I was in high school then, and I doubt my bureau has much on them or the case. But I shall dig around and see what I can find."

*

Lawyers in private practice have to schmooze with potential clients; judges have to be careful who they schmooze with, which made the job perfect for a private man like Jim. He went to his share of extracurricular dinners and events but had a built-in excuse to keep to himself. Now he searched his memory for names of people he knew who might be able to help.

Of the first three people he called, none could give him information about Michael Spinner other than what Jim already knew, and one of the three had no memory of ever meeting Jim.

"Apparently I make an indelible impression," Jim groused to Pat.

Then he recalled a former college classmate, Malcolm Segal, who had done very well in the financial world.

"Yes, I knew Michael Spinner. Quite well in fact," Segal said when Jim called out of the blue.

"Who would want him dead?"

"Lots of people. Take a number."

"At Ryan's sentencing, witness after witness testified as to Spinner's sterling character, his philanthropic work, yet you're telling me a lot of people wanted him dead."

"Spinner was a Jekyll and Hyde type. If he needed you, he oozed charm; if he didn't, you were dreck. Have you talked to his ex-wives?"

"How many wives did he have?""

"Three. Engaged to a fourth, a much younger woman, at the time of his sad demise."

"I remember her from Ryan's trial. Very sincere, as I remember."

"Her name is Pamela Martin. Spinner's women got progressively younger, a few more and 'robbing the cradle' would be a statement of fact."

"Did all his marriages end in divorce?"

"Numbers two and three did. His first wife died. I sat next to number three at a dinner in honor of a mutual friend. She radiated hostility towards Spinner."

"Remember her name?"

"Let me think. Roberta? Robin?"

"Thanks. This has been helpful."

"How have you been, Jim? I see your name in the alumni notes from time to time."

"I do my best to stay out of the alumni notes."

"You never were the social type."

"Nor were you, if I remember."

"I had to learn to be once I entered banking. The rich jealously guard their privacy but love to schmooze with their banker. I had to learn to play golf. *Me*, golf!" Malcolm laughed.

"Any good?"

"Are you kidding? I am the least coordinated man alive. Doesn't matter, it's the schmoozing that matters."

Spinner's second wife had remarried and dropped out of sight. The third, Roberta Spinner, was single and lived in Boston. She expressed no reluctance to meet, in fact she seemed eager to talk about her ex.

They met in the bar of a restaurant called Le Sous-Sol on Newbury Street.

Roberta Spinner was well-mannered, tightly controlled. Narrow face, not a hair out of place. "Pleased to meet you, Judge Randall. You said you had questions about my ex-husband, may the scumbag rest in peace."

The bar was off to the side of the restaurant. A French language broadcast of a tennis match played on TV. Bonjours greeted everyone who walked through the door.

"Yes. The man convicted of his murder is coming up for parole, which made me reflect on what we never learned during his trial."

"Does it matter?"

"To me, it does. One thing about being a judge, you have to confine your reasoning to the facts presented. Now that I'm retired, I'm free to speculate, and I hate unanswered questions. Did you have contact with your ex-husband after he divorced you?"

"As little as possible. He had two daughters by his first wife, who was a lovely woman, and I became close to them, but Michael was a truly reprehensible human being."

"How so?"

"He used my family money to refuel his hedge fund when his luck ran dry, then spit me out like chewing gum. That might be me on the sole of your shoes."

"Did you and he have children?"

"No! Thank God! I wouldn't want to perpetuate his genes."

"But his kids are good people, you said."

"Yes. Two daughters. An evolutionary miracle."

"Where do they live?"

"One in Wellesley, the other in Vermont."

"Would they be willing to talk to me?"

"I'll ask them."

"So who do you think wanted your ex-husband dead?"

"Besides me, you mean? I have no idea. Money didn't make Michael the terrible person he was; there are plenty of benevolent rich people and plenty of assholic poor people. No, Michael Spinner was born with the belief that other people existed solely to serve his needs. He never matured his way out of diapers. I wish I could help you more."

*

Pamela Martin – Michael Spinner's fiancée – had been in her twenties at the time of his death. They were engaged for only a few months. She had made a strong impression on Jim in court – pretty in an understated way, soft-spoken, and very, very sad. Jim remembered her sobbing on the witness stand about her fiancé's death. Martin was still her last name, and she lived in Somerville, not far from The Long Gone.

She answered her phone warily. "Hello?"

"Pamela Martin?"

"Who is this?"

"My name is Jim Randall. I was the judge in Max Ryan's trial."

Silence. "Why are you calling?"

"I retired from the court two years ago. Max Ryan is up for parole and there are unanswered questions in my mind. Would you be willing to talk to me?"

She didn't answer right away, and Jim wondered if she had hung up. Then, she came back on, her voice trembling with emotion. "I don't want to do this over the phone. Can we meet?"

The familiar surroundings of The Long Gone seemed strange to Jim sitting across from a woman he remembered from a murder trial. She was in her mid-to late forties now, with the look of someone who gave little attention to her appearance other than to brush her hair in the morning before she left the house. Once upon a time ready for anything, now jaded but eager to be eager again. He liked her instantly.

"I appreciate your agreeing to meet with me. I could tell over the phone that your former-fiancé's death is still painful to you."

She spoke with understated precision. "Even though I have been married to my husband John for eighteen years, yes, Michael's death is still painful. I was young when he was murdered. The shock of it changed me permanently."

"How did you two meet?"

"I was a grad student in economics, Michael was a guest lecturer for a series on changes in the investment world. I found him fascinating. We had coffee after one of his lectures and found we had a lot to say to each other. I admit I was immediately taken by his self-confidence. His marriage was coming apart, and we fell in love." She shrugged. "I know, I know. Cliche. But it happens."

"Did you know he had been married three times?"

"Yes, but I didn't care."

"Did he express any worries about his hedge fund?"

She answered carefully. "He never talked about his work. He was remarkably upbeat from the moment we met until the day he died."

"Any threats against him that you know of?"

"None." She shook her head. "Keep in mind that I only knew him for a few months, and there was much I didn't know about him. I have since learned that some people interpreted his self-confidence as arrogance and hated him for it, but I found him charming. I had never had anyone pay such close attention to me."

"Have you had any contact with either of the ex-wives who are still alive?"

"No. I reached out to his third wife, Roberta, after the trial. She seemed nice, but she wouldn't meet with me."

"Did she give a reason?"

"Said she felt sorry for me and didn't want to spoil my memories."

"Forgive me, I have no right to ask this, but do you now have any regrets about becoming engaged to Michael Spinner?"

"No regrets but amazement I was so naive. I hardly knew him. I still don't know why I leapt so quickly. Youth, inexperience with older men, unresolved issues with my father?"

Jim nodded. "I had no right to ask."

"My turn. Do your questions mean you think Max Ryan wasn't Michael's killer?"

"My questions mean I don't think we know everything about the murder. I was inexperienced as a judge, and in retirement I've had chances to second-guess myself. I'm probably wrong to do so but I can't help myself. Anything else you can remember about that evening?"

"I remember that Michael seemed wistful. He talked about our relationship as if he were fondly remembering a relationship that had ended long ago. We ate at the Fish and Fowl, his favorite restaurant which he usually loved, but he came close to tears once or twice."

She faltered. "Take your time," Jim said.

"He fell so ill in the cab going home that I had the cab take us to the hospital. He died during the night."

"I'm very sorry to bring this all back to you."

"It's never far from my mind."

"You say he fell ill in the cab? Did he seem ill during dinner?"

"No. Sad, nostalgic, but not ill."

"Did anyone approach him during dinner?"

"Only the waitstaff. Michael ate there frequently and the staff took wonderful care of him." She paused. "Judge Randall, I would hate to think the wrong person has been in prison all these years."

*

Jim and Pat stayed at Jim's that night and ate around the corner at their favorite restaurant, Duck, Duck, Goose.

Bruce, the co-owner, greeted them at the door. "Haven't seen you two for what...?"

"Six days?" Jim said.

"Where have you been?"

"Beacon Hill. Another country."

"Your table is ready."

He showed them to their usual table in the corner by the front window. It was a table for four, but Bruce saved it for them except during Harvard Commencement Week, when Cambridge restaurants were full to bursting with proud Harvard parents.

Duck, Duck, Goose had an excellent wine list. Jim ordered a Coteaux du Languedoc that was slightly more expensive than his usual.

"This doesn't taste familiar," Pat said when the wine was poured.

"We've never had it before. Do you like it?"

"Jammy."

He laughed. "Since when did you learn wine speak?"

"Never. I have no idea what jammy means, I just like the word. How did your meeting with Pamela Martin go?"

"I think she can be helpful."

"Meaning she was good looking?"

"Excuse me?"

"Never mind. She can be helpful. Go on."

"Good looking in a very married way, my dear. You have a warped opinion of me."

Pat smiled indulgently. "Yes. Continue."

"Married for many years now to a man named John. She didn't have time to get to know Michael Spinner well, but meeting with her made me wonder who got Spinner's money when he died?"

"Did Ryan's defense attorney raise the issue during the trial?"

"Tried to, but I excluded Spinner's will as evidence on the grounds that Max Ryan was on trial, not Michael Spinner." Jim paused. "Maybe Ted Conover knows."

"Jim, that was a long time ago, and Ted was a very junior ADA."

"Which is why he may have been assigned the grunt work. I'll call him tomorrow."

*

Jim had to speak loudly to be heard over the traffic noise. "Who did Michael Spinner leave his money to?"

"You expect me to remember that far back?"

"Yes, I do. A man of your brilliance."

Ted and Jim were walking from Ted's office to the courthouse, the only time Ted could fit Jim in. Jim liked the neighborhoods near the courthouse, some of them quaint, some of them ramshackle.

Ted sensed his mood. "Feeling nostalgic for your old 'hood?'"

Jim smiled. "Not enough to regret retiring."

"I was brand new in the DA's office when Spinner was murdered, and a lot about his trial is a blur. What I remember is that traces of arsenic found on Max Ryan's clothes quickly pointed at Ryan as Spinner's killer, and a newly hired line cook reported seeing Ryan sprinkle what looked like powder on Spinner's semifreddo before it was carried into the dining room. The line cook died in an auto accident after the trial, so you can't interview him, if that's what this is leading up to. Max Ryan vehemently denied the line cook's testimony but couldn't explain how the arsenic got on his clothes. The rest, as they say, is history."

"Were you convinced of Ryan's guilt?"

"I was at the time. I see skepticism in your eyes. What are you thinking?"

"It was my first murder trial as a judge, and I didn't know what I was doing, but I remember wishing the evidence were more conclusive."

"I felt much the same way. I fear I had more zeal than wisdom early in my prosecutorial career. One thing that bothered me was lack of motive. We explored money as a motive and found that Spinner's will left only a small amount to his children, and none to his ex-wives – or Max Ryan, who he didn't know – so his will was not introduced as evidence."

"Who got the bulk of his money?"

"Not who. What. The bulk of his estate was to be left to a foundation named after none other than Michael Spinner. The Spinner Foundation. Heard of it?"

"No."

"That's because it died when Spinner did. Guess who was tentatively named to head the foundation if it had become a reality?"

"His fiancée, Pamela Martin."

"Yes, but as I said, it never got off the ground. Spinner failed to get it going before he died. I have no idea what happened to Spinner's money after his death."

"So no one benefitted financially from his death?"

"As far as I know. Which is why we never raised it as a motive at Max Ryan's trial."

4

The Spinner daughter who lived in Wellesley refused to see Jim or talk to him. "I have put my father's murder behind me," she told him, "and I don't want to revisit it." The daughter who lived in Vermont was willing to meet with him.

She lived in Dorset, and her name was Julie.

"What do you expect to find?" Pat asked Jim as they drove up for the weekend.

"I don't know. Hints, clues. Dorset is a fancy town. Her father didn't leave her much when he died, so she must have money of her own."

"Is she married?"

"Her last name is Fisher, so I assume she is or was married."

They stopped at Jim's house overlooking the Connecticut River for the night. Stale air leapt up to greet them like an eager puppy when they opened the door. It had been longer than usual since their last visit.

They ate dinner at the house, went to bed early, and the next morning drove across state to Dorset and the meeting with Julie Fisher.

She greeted them in the front parlor of her modest home. She appeared to be in her thirties. She sat them down in her front parlor and brought them coffee.

"Did you just drive up?"

"No, we drove up yesterday. We have a house north of Brattleboro."

"My husband Jake grew up in Brattleboro," Julie said. "His father was an aging hippie, Jake is anything but. He likes Vermont but wanted nothing to do with Brattleboro's Sixties vibe when he was old enough to move away."

"How long have you lived in Dorset?"

"Three years. Before that in Weston, outside of Boston. Jake is a financial advisor. After he did well in a big firm he wanted to strike out on his own, and he started a small practice here. He loves every second of it."

"As I understand it, you and your sister are the children of your father's first marriage, but I don't know where you grew up."

"In Newton, which you know if you're from the Boston area. When my mother died, my father moved us to the North Shore, which I hated."

"How do you and Roberta Spinner get along?"

"By her choice I rarely see her, but I liked her the few times I have. She was too nice for Dad. Their divorce wasn't her fault. Dad always thought there was someone better than the woman he was with."

"Which makes me wonder about his engagement to Pamela Martin, whom I have met. Do you know her well?"

"Barely at all. Dad died before I could get to know her."

"She is happily married but still saddened by your dad's death."

"Really?"

"You sound surprised."

"If she had time to know him better, she wouldn't be as sad. I loved Dad best from a distance."

"Was that because he was a bad father, or because he was a bad man?"

Julie stood. "Would you like more coffee?"

"No, I'm fine. Pat?"

"I'm fine too," Pat said.

"Be right back." Julie disappeared in back.

Pat whispered to Jim. "Tread gently, Jim. She's vulnerable."

"She seems put together to me."

"Her father wounded her somehow. She's come to terms with it and carries on admirably, but be careful."

Julie returned, her coffee cup refilled. "Much better," she said, placing the full cup on the side table next to her chair. "I'll answer your question. Dad constructed a self for others to see. He was a master showman. My sister and I glimpsed the real Dad, but even we had no clue, that's how good a conjurer he was. Whenever my sister or I tried to peek beneath the surface, Dad became livid. We quickly learned to give him ample room. He was a delight to be around as long as we treated his false front as the real Dad."

"How did you and your sister feel when he left Roberta?"

"I felt terrible for her, but Roberta had her act together, and we knew she'd do fine. I sensed she had discovered the real Dad and that's why he left her."

"Did you ever talk to her about what went wrong?"

"She refused to tell me. Said it was for my own good."

"Your father's will left little to you and your sister. That must have hurt."

"No, he talked to us about it ahead of time. When it came to money, he was blunt. Said we had to earn our own. He believed that inheriting a lot of money could ruin a person."

"He set up a foundation. What was its purpose?"

"To fund research into the genetic basis for anxiety and depression. Dad was super confident in public, but in rare unguarded moments after Mom died, anxiety and fear would leak from his pores. He was afraid of losing everything and having to start over."

"Was that even conceivably possible? Wasn't he worth billions?"

Julie shrugged. "We thought so too, but his lawyer told us that given the massive amount of debt that Dad acquired before his death, he died essentially broke."

"Interesting. Do you think that had anything to do with his death?"

Julie's eyes narrowed. "How do you mean?"

"Could a client have tried to redeem his shares and found that your dad couldn't pay him what he was owed? That could drive even a gentle soul over the edge."

"If that happened, I wasn't privy to it, but furious at Dad? Lots of people were, client and non-client alike. If Dad didn't want to charm someone, he could be flagrantly obnoxious."

"Obnoxious enough to make someone want to kill him?"

Her voice turned to ice. "Of course not. I can think of no earthly reason why someone would want to kill Dad, as obnoxious as he could be. You don't kill obnoxious people, you say bad things about them on social media. Now if you'll excuse me."

"I'm sorry if I crossed a line. You've been very helpful."

Jim and Pat left Dorset soon after. "So, what did you think of her?" Jim asked as they drove east across the state.

"I liked her. She will outlast her enemies, if she has any," Pat said.

"Did you see the way she closed down at the end?"

"I didn't blame her. You were not gentle."

"Do you think she's hiding something, or do you think certain things are too painful for her to think about?"

"The latter. I don't think she knows more than she lets on."

Vermont has hills and mountains to spare: the Greens, the Taconics. Flat land wider than a few corn fields is rare. Jim liked the rise and fall of driving across state. He reached his house on the border content with the journey if not what he had gleaned from Julie.

He opened the door and stepped aside to let Pat enter. As she did, he asked, "What did you make of the fact that Michael Spinner was essentially broke when he died?"

"I wonder if he died broke because he made bad investment decisions for his hedge fund, or had he been running a Ponzi scheme all along?"

"Same here, but for my purposes in deciding whether to support Max Ryan's parole, it doesn't matter why Spinner died broke, just that he did."

"I disagree. Spinner's pride was at stake. If he had run a Ponzi scheme, he would be remembered as a criminal. If he had made bad investment decisions, he'd look like a failed hedge fund manager, but could salvage a little bit of pride."

"What's that have to do with his death?"

"Don't discount the role of pride, is what I'm saying."

"Pat, you are becoming more cryptic with age."

Jim turned on the light in the kitchen and opened a bottle of Samur. He could tell it had corked as soon as he opened it, but to be sure, he took a sip. The face he made was a living emoji.

"Ruined?" Pat asked.

"Slaughtered," he replied. "Let's eat out."

*

Before they returned to Boston, Jim invited Roberta Spinner to join them for dinner at Le Sous-Sol when they got back. They got back the following day, and went straight to the restaurant. Roberta had arrived when they got there, but their table wasn't ready, so the three of them had a drink in the slender adjacent bar. Jim raised his glass. "To justice."

The wine was assertive.

Glasses were lowered. Jim thanked Roberta for arranging the meeting with Julie Fisher. "She had a lot to say, some of which raised questions you might be able to answer."

"I told you everything I know."

"Julie speculated that her father left you because you saw him for what he was."

Roberta scoffed. "He left me because he found a younger woman, as was his wont. Julie was infatuated with her dad. Cuckoo about him. She resented me the whole time Michael and I were married. She's a very intelligent woman who shielded herself from the truth about her dad as long as she could."

"Interesting. She didn't speak ill of you or talk about him with adoration."

"Revisionist thinking on her part."

"Was she at least right that you saw through him? Did you discover some disturbing secret about him?"

"I told you. He was an ass, but it was no secret."

The dining room off the bar was busy without seeming crowded. The waiters were all good-looking. Pat, Roberta, and Jim were seated at a front table.

"What's good here?" Roberta said, perusing the menu.

"Lemon sole," Pat said.

"Steak frites," Jim said.

"I'll have the coq au vin," Roberta told the waiter, snapping her menu shut. "When Michael left me for Pamela Martin, I hated her guts but came to feel grateful. She took Michael off my hands."

Jim said, "When I talked to her she didn't seem his type. When they met, she must have seemed the innocent. No match for a twice-married man like him."

Roberta gave Jim a skeptical look. "Judge Randall, perhaps you were shielded by your robe from men like Michael. They fall for whoever can boost their egos or be helpful to them at the moment. That is their 'type.' Pamela came along at a time when Michael's reputation was taking a hit and he needed a fresh young thing by his side. Pamela filled the bill."

"Then why would he make her the head of the Spinner Foundation?" Jim asked.

"Good question. I don't know. One possibility: men like Michael are mush at the core and maybe he truly fell for her. If so, believe me, it wouldn't have lasted. Second possibility: it was a tax dodge. Possibility number three: he wanted her to believe he admired her for more than her looks and youth, so he wrote her into his will as the head of a sham foundation. I wouldn't put it past Michael to show Pamela his will to persuade her to marry him, without ever intending to fund the foundation."

"I think you're close." Jim had felt some sympathy for her the first time they met, but now he sensed that she could be every bit as self-regarding as her ex, but that didn't mean she was wrong about the kind of man he was.

She marveled at the coq au vin. "Very Parisian," she murmured.

"Do you know Paris?"

"Oh, yes, very well. Michael and I traveled there two or three times." Roberta wanted dessert. "How's the chocolate mousse here?"

"Standard," Pat replied.

"I'll have that," Roberta said with relish.

It was a nice evening, and Jim and Pat chose to walk to Cambridge across the Mass Ave bridge when dinner was over. The #1 bus plied Mass Ave, so they could jump on a bus if they tired. The Charles River is wide at that point, affording expansive views of Boston and Cambridge's low profiles. Jim listened to his footsteps.

"She is a brittle woman," Pat said.

"I realized that tonight," Jim echoed.

A pleasure boat parted the waters between Boston and Cambridge, its wake catching the lights of the cities. The two cities sparkled modestly, as if to not draw undue attention to themselves.

Jim stopped suddenly, so suddenly that Pat had to back up a step. "I've been making too many assumptions."

"What do you mean?"

"Two thoughts come to mind. Did somebody put Max Ryan up to this as I've been assuming or did Ryan have motive to kill Spinner? Secondly, was the forensic evidence presented at the trial as convincing as I believed?"

"Weren't you convinced by what you heard?"

"At the time I was, but now I wonder if I was trying too hard not to mess up my first murder trial."

5

Jim had been operating on the assumption that Max Ryan had no reason to want Michael Spinner dead, therefore someone must have put Ryan up to it. Was that true? A long legal career had taught Jim that assumptions can lead one astray, no matter how airtight the logic that follows. Examine the assumption. Might Max Ryan, a young man from a much different background that Spinner, have harbored a grudge against him? Had Spinner wronged him somehow?

A love affair gone wrong was one possibility. Spinner was relentlessly heterosexual, judging by his marriages and engagement. But those could have been for show, to keep his homosexuality a secret from the macho men of Wall Street. Acceptance of homosexuality was fairly recent, after all, and there still were pockets of resistance in certain professions and communities.

Mitigating against that was the impression Pamela Martin had made on Jim. He could imagine her – young and naive when she met Michael Spinner – ignoring or missing signals that he was gay, but Jim's gut told him that was unlikely. Young, naive he could imagine her being, sexually insensitive, no. There you go, Jim, letting a woman's attractiveness turn your head again. Shove a broken love affair between Spinner and Ryan as the motive for murder to the back of your mind, but don't toss it into the recycling bin just yet.

The Long Gone was the place for stray thoughts and daydreams, the place where ideas would pop into Jim's mind unbidden. He walked there one morning while he was on his 'who was Max Ryan' kick and barely had sat down with his dark roast when he changed his mind about talking to Max Ryan's wife a second time. Leaving his coffee on the table beside his Boston *Globe*, he went to the sidewalk and called the number she had left with him when she approached him in The Long Gone and asked for help with her husband's parole.

"Hello?" She answered on the eighth ring.

"Deborah Ryan?"

Without hesitation, she agreed to meet.

The meeting place was The Long Gone – full circle. He had forgotten what she looked like. A woman in her forties, haggard but kind face. She spoke with traces of a Boston accent.

"I didn't expect to hear from you," she said.

"I didn't expect to call."

"What changed your mind?"

"After you asked for my help, I thought about your husband's trial. If I had it to do over, I'd insist on a more thorough explanation of the why of the murder before I passed judgement. If I knew the why, I think I'd be certain of the who. I passed judgement having too many unanswered questions in my mind."

She visibly relaxed. "I'm relieved. Thank you, thank you."

"Don't get your hopes up. I'm probably the worst person to look into your husband's case; my ego has a vested interest in proving I was right."

"I believe you are a fair man, Judge."

Jim shook his head. "Thank you, but actually I'm ornery and opinionated." He watched her closely. "Tell me about your husband."

"He's a good man, Judge Randall. Even after all these years in prison, he isn't bitter. I would be, but not Max. He doesn't hold grudges, he just wants to get out."

"He could make that more likely by expressing remorse. That's what has prevented his parole until now."

"How can he express remorse for something he didn't do? Tell me that, Judge Randall."

Jim had to admit that point had occurred to him and was one of the reasons he had mentally reopened the case, but he didn't say that to Deborah Ryan. "As far as you know, did he have any reason to hate Michael Spinner?"

"None."

"Did he know Spinner?"

"By name and dessert preference, yes. The owner of the Fish and Fowl, Teddy Demarco, wanted Max to prepare Mr. Spinner's favorite dessert whenever he came in. Max used to complain to me that it was an awful lot of extra work just to please one guy, but Teddy said that Mr. Spinner was an important customer, and to give him what he wants. As far as I know, Max never spoke to Mr. Spinner. Complained about having to make Meyer lemon semifreddo again and again, but never spoke to him."

"Did your husband complain about other customers?"

"Max grew up in a rough neighborhood and learned swagger out of necessity, but at heart, he's a gentle man. He escaped his neighborhood as soon as he could and believed in treating everybody with respect, giving them great food and excellent service, and minding his own business."

"Did your husband get along with the owner?"

Deborah hesitated. "Not really. Teddy sucked up to the customers but treated the kitchen staff like dirt. Max hated to be pushed around, and Teddy was straight out of reality television, cursing, shoving."

"So, Teddy Demarco was a bully and your husband hated being bullied. Could that have contributed to Michael Spinner's death?"

"I don't see how. In what way?"

"Perhaps Max resented the special treatment Teddy Demarco lavished on Spinner and blamed Spinner."

"Nonsense. Max isn't the kind of man to take out his anger at the owner on a customer. And he shied away from violence. He had learned how to swagger, but when he wasn't being pushed around, he was the gentlest of men." Deborah Ryan reddened. "Max doesn't stand a chance of being paroled, does he, Judge Randall? You sent him to prison, you're not going to watch him go free." She stood from the table. "I'm sorry to have bothered you."

"You haven't bothered me at all. To the contrary, I'm glad you spoke up. Please stay."

She left The Long Gone before he could say more.

Jim felt terrible. He walked home the long way, past the live poultry store and Beauty Shop Row, but still felt terrible when he got home. Max Ryan had spent twenty years in prison and his wife had stuck by him, and Jim had drained her of hope. He mentally slapped himself for clumsiness in the first degree.

"It doesn't sound so bad to me," Pat replied when he told her of his encounter.

"Really?"

"It sounds like the kind of questions you might have asked from the bench."

"But I'm no longer on the bench. I've run out of excuses. I have to meet Max Ryan."

*

The visiting room had a long partitioned table and uncomfortable metal chairs. Jim was familiar with prison visiting rooms and found all of them eerily similar. Chilly, bleak. Would it hurt to paint the walls a vibrant color, have chairs that didn't hurt the spine? Was the idea to punish the visitor as well as the prisoner?

Jim had little memory of Ryan's appearance from the trial twenty years ago. Even if he did, he doubted he'd recognize the man sitting across the table. Max Ryan had aged badly. He seemed to have no idea at first who Jim was, then remembered. "I know you." His voice fit his wife's description of him as a gentle man.

"Yes, I was the judge in your trial."

"Did Deborah talk to you? Is that why you're here?"

"She talked to me because you're up for parole and she asked for my help. She didn't tell you?"

"No." Ryan leaned back, not an easy thing to do in the metal chairs. "I should hate you."

"You don't?"

"Never did. You were just doing your job. I didn't feel the same way about the DA and the jury."

"I'll get to the point. I was a young and inexperienced judge when I heard your case, and if I made mistakes I want to correct them."

"You're going to speak up for me?"

Jim shook his head. "Too early to say. All I promise at this point is that I'm looking into your case."

Ryan peered over Jim's shoulder. "That's something at least."

"Help me understand. You haven't expressed remorse in all the years since the trial. If you expressed remorse now, you would have a much better chance of parole."

"I grew up stubborn, Judge Randall, and there's no way in hell I'm going to confess to a crime I didn't commit. How could I live with myself?"

"Your wife would love to have you home."

Ryan's expression eased. "And I would love to be home with her, make no mistake. She has stuck with me all these years. But in the end, honor is all a man has, the only thing he can take to his grave."

"Help me understand. During my career as a judge I sentenced many people to prison. Most didn't protest their innocence once the trial was over, but a few – like you – did. Some, I'm reasonably sure, simply couldn't bring themselves to admit the horrible things they had done. But you seem different to me. Can you explain to me what makes you willing to stay in prison rather than admit your guilt?"

"Because I'm innocent! I didn't kill anybody. Would you admit to being a murderer if you hadn't killed anyone? Simple as that."

"I might weigh the prospect of freedom versus the momentary shame of saying 'I'm guilty'."

"There would be nothing momentary about it. Forever after that, I'd be branded in my own mind, and others, as a confessed killer. I couldn't live with that."

Jim was satisfied that Ryan believed what he was saying. "Mr. Ryan, I've been pushing you to see if there was any give in your position. I'm satisfied you are telling the truth, as far as you see the truth. Now, can you answer a few questions to satisfy my lingering doubts about your trial?"

Ryan seemed perplexed. Was the judge tricking him? "Go ahead," he said.

"Take me through the process of preparing Michael Spinner's favorite dessert. Did anyone help you prepare his Meyer lemon semifreddo?"

"Never. Only me. Mr. Spinner insisted he could tell my semifreddo from other people's, and Teddy Demarco wanted to keep Mr. Spinner happy."

"You were the assistant pastry chef. The pastry chef never made the semifreddo?"

"Not Mr. Spinner's. The pastry chef wouldn't dare make Teddy Demarco angry. Besides, Mondays were her night off. She wasn't at the restaurant the night Mr. Spinner died."

"Michael Spinner died of arsenic poisoning on the way home from the restaurant. Traces of arsenic were found on your clothes. Since arsenic wasn't found elsewhere in the kitchen, a reasonable assumption is that you put arsenic in the dessert you prepared for him that night."

"But I didn't."

"So how did the arsenic get on your clothes and no one else's?"

"I have no idea. You're asking me to solve a crime I didn't commit."

"But the circumstances make you look bad, don't you admit?"

"Of course. But it's never been my job to prove who killed Spinner. That was the job of the DA."

"The jury found you guilty."

Ryan gave the kind of shrug Jim had seen from other convicts who have been worn to a nub by prison. "Juries have been wrong before."

"Could someone from outside have gotten into the kitchen and slipped poison into the semifreddo?"

"No, sir. I was always watchful of my work, and Chef Anders was like a general preparing his troops for battle."

"Anders was the head chef?"

Ryan nodded. "Olaf Anders. He was brutal about detail. Everything had to be perfect or pots would fly."

"He was questioned extensively before and during the trial and seemed devastated by what happened. Did you get along with him?"

"No, but I respected his talent as a chef. He had plans to open his own restaurant. What happened to him, do you know?"

"I don't, but I should. Did you know Michael Spinner?"

"Only as a regular who loved Meyer lemon semifreddo. When he started seeing Pamela Martin, he would bring her sometimes. I knew Pamela from high school. We grew up together."

"Oh? Did you know her well?"

"No, just from school. We didn't hang out together or anything like that. Her parents were educated, and Pamela was raised with advantages I didn't have, but she was always nice to me. Said hello to me in the hall, that kind of thing. She left our school in tenth grade to go to prep school."

"You must have been surprised to see her when she first showed up at the Fish and Fowl."

"Not really. I knew she would do well for herself. Very smart, very driven."

"Was she ever your girlfriend?"

"Pamela?" Ryan didn't laugh often, judging by the set of his face, but he laughed loudly now.

"I take it the answer is no?"

"Pamela was nice to me, but never in a million years would she go out with me."

"How can you be sure of that?"

"Judge Randall, I can tell you didn't know Southie back then. It was unusual for someone from Pamela's neighborhood to be nice to someone from mine, let alone go out with them."

A prison guard gestured to Jim that it was time to go. "I've got to leave, Mr. Ryan. No promises. You may or may not hear from me again."

"I'm innocent, Judge. No offense, but you and the jury made a mistake. I've spent twenty years of my life in here for something I didn't do."

*

Jim brooded for days after his visit with Max Ryan. Prison makes all men seem like liars and crooks, and Max Ryan in prison was no exception, but Jim found Ryan to be generally credible. He based that assessment on over twenty years of assessing the credibility of witnesses. The law is based on reason – as well it should be – but reason is a blunt instrument, ill suited to judge human nature, and that's what a trial is: flawed humans judging other flawed humans. It was astounding there weren't more mistakes.

When Jim got into one of his funks, Pat gave him ample room. It was no good to coax or cajole, no good to look on the bright side. When Jim got into one of his funks, there were no bright sides. Let the man brood.

At dinnertime on the fourth day, Jim came out of his funk. They were in Pat's kitchen on Beacon Hill.

"Hello," she said. "Where have you been?"

"Imagining what it would be like to be in prison for twenty years if I were innocent." He noticed his food, untouched until now. He took a forkful. "Would it be like locked-in syndrome, where one is conscious but can't move or speak?"

"You're talking about Max Ryan, I presume. Didn't his wife visit him in prison?"

"You're so literal. Yes, his wife visited him. Why didn't his attorney give the prosecution a harder time for not proving motive? Ted didn't prosecute the case, by the way, he was too new in the DA's office."

"Did Ryan testify at the trial?"

"No. His attorney refused to let him. His attorney gambled that the prosecution hadn't proved its case and refused to let Ryan testify on his own behalf. I thought then that was a risky choice, and having talked with Ryan now, I'm even more convinced of it."

"Jim, you believe him now, but you don't know what impression he would have made on the jury."

Jim looked stunned. "You know what? Ryan has spent almost as many years in prison as I served on the bench."

"Don't, Jim."

He sprang to his feet. "I feel sick. I'm going to get some air. No need for you to come."

Pat rose. "Are you kidding? When you're in this mood, you're likely to get hit by a car."

They walked downhill toward Charles Street. They didn't get far before Jim stubbed his toe on the brick sidewalk. He exhaled loudly and raised his eyes. A slice of the Charles River could be seen between the buildings. "I need to calm down, don't I?"

"I think so."

He regained his balance. "The alternative would be to curl up in a fetal position and roll down the hill."

"Not advisable."

They continued walking. Dusk sheltered them. "I'm sure the Ryan case is not the only mistake I made in twenty-one years on the bench."

"You're assuming you made a mistake in the Ryan case."

"But let's assume I did. Every judge makes mistakes, right? I shouldn't take this one so personally."

"Why have you?"

Jim shook his head. "No idea. Maybe Deborah Ryan approaching me at The Long Gone? Or maybe talking to Max Ryan in prison. Never before have I visited a man I sent to prison."

Pat said, "Come to think of it, in all the years I was on the bench, I never did either."

"Maybe that should be obligatory for new judges. Visit the first ten prisoners you sentence."

They approached the base of the hill. She took his hand. "Careful, this is where you might walk into traffic if you were by yourself."

He shot her a look. "I am too cautious a man to do that. But hang on tight to my hand, just in case."

6

The Fish and Fowl had undergone several permutations since Michael Spinner's death. After a succession of owners tried without success to latch on to the food trend du jour, a brash young owner restored the restaurant to its original shabby grandeur. Old Money, having no place to go after Locke-Ober and the Ritz-Carlton closed, now had their clubhouse back. The key to appealing to Old Money was to look opulent but not shiny (e.g., the paintings on the wall of quail and carp should look as if they were purchased at a yard sale; when a serving cart chips paint on the swinging kitchen door, leave the chipped paint as a symbol of longevity) and no matter how much you modernize the menu, make sure to include a few stalwarts like Dover sole, roast chicken, and prime rib.

It wasn't Jim and Pat's kind of place, but Jim wanted to get a sense of the room now so they made a reservation. Once they were seated, Pat asked, "I hate this place. It could use a fresh coat of paint and an airing out. Do you like it?"

"Not particularly, but I get its appeal."

"Do you want to explain it to me?"

"A spiffy place would attract those who haven't been rich long enough for their money to marinate. Old Money values restraint, discretion. New Money is the monetary equivalent of a flasher."

"Michael Spinner ate here," Pat said. "He wasn't Old Money."

"He was halfway between Old and New. He knew how to pass as one of them briefly."

"You act like you knew him."

"I'm getting to know him. Speculate with me about the night he was poisoned. He was eating here with his fiancé. Assume you are Pamela Martin and I am Spinner. What was special about the night?"

"Could it have been the night they set a date for their wedding?"

"I don't know why that would have led to his murder."

Pat looked askance at him. "You asked me to speculate, I'm speculating."

"I'm sorry. Go on."

"Maybe it was the night Spinner told Pamela he had revised his will to set up a foundation for her to run. Then again, why would that lead to his death?"

"Good question. How about this for a possibility? Max Ryan said he knew Pamela Martin in high school. Although he denied having any involvement with her, maybe Max Ryan and Pamela had been lovers, and maybe she revealed that to Spinner that night."

"Why would that lead to Spinner's death?"

"It wouldn't. Unless...."

"Unless what?"

"Follow me here, what if Pamela said she and Max Ryan had started sleeping with each other again, which drove Spinner into a rage, which then led him to confront Ryan, which led to Ryan killing Spinner."

Pat stared at Jim in amused silence.

"What? Are you implying with that look that I have gone stark raving mad?"

"Mildly deranged."

"Okay, so we have no idea what, if anything, happened that night that led to Spinner's murder. To our brilliance." He lifted his wine glass in a toast.

After dinner, they walked the short distance to the Red Line. The maze-like back streets of the business district were quiet at night. Ghosts seemed to dwell in the alleyways. Jim took Pat's hand.

"You've done that twice in recent memory. Keep it up and I might get used to it." Pat glanced at him as they walked.

"Don't feel singled out. I hold hands with anyone who will speculate with me."

"If you really want to impress me, you could put your arm around me."

"Here? Where the tourists could see?"

"What tourists? There's no one else on the street."

"Keep your voice down. Ghosts have ears, you know."

She walked a few steps in silence. "If the folks in your courtroom had known what the gruff man on the bench was like off it, your robe would have been no shield."

"Quiet, woman."

A few more steps in silence. "Jim, do you think Michael Spinner really cared for Pamela Martin?"

"She cared for him, I know that much. She remains shaken by his murder, even after all these years."

"But older man, younger woman? Isn't that classic?"

"Spinner wasn't that much older than Pamela."

"Spoken like a senior citizen."

"Look who's talking."

"I'm not sixty-five yet."

"What are you? Sixty-three?"

"You don't know?"

"You're sixty-three."

"I'm sixty-four."

"Too old for me."

The subway took forever to arrive and then halted between Kendall and Central Squares for a reason that sounded like "hominy grits" over the faulty loudspeaker. When Jim and Pat exited at Harvard Square, the fresh(er) air felt especially welcome.

"Here's my thinking so far," Jim said as they walked the few blocks to his townhouse. "My guess is that Spinner's hedge fund had suffered major losses and that he set up the foundation as a way to shield what was left of his assets. Foundations aren't taxed as much as individuals."

"Do you think Pamela Martin knew about his losses?"

"I don't think she had a clue about Spinner's finances. He was very good at shielding who he was from prying eyes. And Pamela was too dazzled by him to pry."

They reached Jim's townhouse. He climbed the few steps and unlocked the front door. "I have more questions for Pamela Martin. I want to meet with her again."

*

Jim met Pamela Martin at The Long Gone, as he had the first time. She seemed glad to see him. "Does this meeting mean you've found something?"

"I'm afraid not. At least not any final answers. But my doubts remain about Max Ryan being the one who wanted Michael Spinner dead. If I could prove he wasn't, would you be inclined to support his parole?"

"You're asking me to do something very hard."

"Max told me you were nice to him in high school."

She seemed shocked. "He told you that?"

"In prison, when I visited him. Is it true?"

"Yes it's true, but I didn't realize you had spoken to him."

Jim nodded. "After much thought, I decided I had to."

"What did he say about me?"

"That you knew each other in high school, and that you were nice to him even though you grew up in different neighborhoods of Southie. He denied any involvement with you other than that."

She scoffed. "Of course there was no other involvement. Do you mean sex?"

"I have to explore every possibility."

Her expression became fierce. "Max seemed genuine and shy with girls. I liked him enough to cross the divide between cliques in school. I said hello to him in the halls, that sort of thing. Whether I had sex with him or anyone else is none of your business."

"I'm sorry."

"But I didn't. I escaped high school with my virginity intact. Is that what you wanted to know?"

"I'm sorry, really I am, that's not what I meant. I blundered into this line of questioning trying to rule out jealousy as a factor."

The Long Gone had few patrons that morning. A man who looked like he lived on the streets slouched at a rear table, mumbling to himself. A student-age young man with a smile on his face avidly studied his phone.

"Before Michael's death, did he give any indication he was in serious financial trouble?"

"I knew he had hit a rough patch, but he was always upbeat when he was with me." Her eyes became suspicious again. "In case you're wondering, I wasn't after Michael's money. In spite of what you and anyone else thinks, I loved Michael, and he loved me. He told me he intended to set up some sort of foundation in his will for me to run if he died before me, but nothing came of it. I wasn't after Michael's money."

"I believe you."

Jim walked home drawing a mental picture of Michael Spinner and Pamela Martin. Spinner was a driven man with a nasty streak who could be charming when it was to his advantage. Pamela Martin was young and gullible and eager to love when she met Spinner. Jim didn't doubt she loved him and wasn't after his money.

He needed to know more about Spinner's money. He called Sasha Cohen of the *Globe*. They met early the next morning at a café in downtown Boston.

"This will have to be brief," she said. "I have a meeting with the governor at eight."

"Big story?"

"Front page, if what I've learned so far holds true."

"Then I especially appreciate your taking the time for me."

"Jim, if it weren't for you, I'd probably still be working for a weekly. What's up?"

"Remember I told you that the man convicted of Michael Spinner's murder is up for parole?"

"You expressed doubts about the verdict, if I remember."

"I expressed doubts we knew the whole story. It was my first murder trial. I didn't know what I was doing, so I carefully followed the rules, but that's not necessarily how one arrives at a correct verdict."

Her phone rang. She checked her messages. "The governor's press secretary wants to know if I can get there by 7:45."

"I'll make this quick. I'd like to know more about Michael Spinner's business dealings in the months before he died. I know that was long ago, but will you check Spinner's file at the *Globe*? This was a high profile killing of one of the new breed of financial wizards so it received a lot of attention at the time."

"I'll see what we've got. But what do you have? You've learned something or you wouldn't be asking."

"I talked to Max Ryan in prison. It is hard for me to imagine him on his own dreaming up the scheme to poison Spinner, especially at the Fish and Fowl where Max would be an obvious suspect. Somebody more skilled in murder put him up to it. Max may not have even known what he was doing."

Sasha mulled that for a minute, then checked the time. "Got to go, Jim, but I've learned that your instincts are good. I'll dig in our files and see what I can find."

"Concentrate on Spinner's finances: public filings, bankruptcies, any lawsuits against him or his hedge fund. I want to know as much as I can about his financial health at the time he died. And thanks, Sasha. Thanks very much."

*

Here's what Sasha discovered: a year before Spinner's death, a man named Cullen sued Spinner claiming his hedge fund had committed fraud in its presentation to investors. The case was settled out of court and the settlement sealed by court order. Cullen had since died.

In a second case, a wealthy widow named Anderson sued Spinner for failure to distribute earnings, and in the third and most significant case, a pension fund for retired teachers sued Spinner's fund for negligence and won.

"The second case was the one that brought Spinner's fund to its knees," Sasha told Jim over coffee at The Long Gone. "From that point on, investors were extremely reluctant to trust him with their money. The only thing that prevented all the investors from pulling their money out were the substantial penalties for early withdrawal built into the investment agreements. As it was, the fund was on life support." Sasha looked across the table at Jim. "Is that what you wanted to know?"

"It's exactly what I wanted to know," Jim replied. "Thank you."

"What does it tell you about Spinner's murder?"

"That Spinner's hedge fund was not the robust earnings machine he claimed it to be. What remains to be seen is whether Spinner was an inept money manager or it was a Ponzi-type scheme from the beginning."

Jim was startled by a male barista shouting, "Heather! Mocha almond latte!" Jim nodded in the barista's direction. "Must be a new guy. Way too loud."

*

How many times in a typical case did Jim think of packing it in? His modus vivendi was to plunge in where he didn't belong, get wrapped up in solving someone else's puzzle, then doubt he had a clue about how to solve it. So it was now. Solving a puzzle and all-hope-is-lost were joined at the hip, he had long since learned.

"Ready to give up?" Pat asked him that night at a semi-dive they hadn't tried before called the Wink and Nod. Pat had decided they were spending too much money on restaurant meals, so suggested this low-cost alternative to Duck, Duck, Goose.

The Wink and Nod was halfway to The Long Gone and shared its gloomy lighting. Sitting in the semi-darkness, Jim compared the similarities between the curated shabbiness of an upscale place like the Fish and Fowl and the happenstance shabbiness of a neighborhood hangout like the Wink and Nod.

"Jim, are you listening? I asked, are you ready to give up on Max Ryan?"

Jim shook himself back to attention. "You know me better than that."

"To remind you, the man has already served time and nothing you do can change that. Sometimes, Jim, your unwillingness to admit defeat is stubbornness, not strength."

Jim bristled. "Maybe I'm being selfish. Maybe the only reason I care is to prove to myself I didn't screw up my first murder trial. Okay?"

Pat gave Jim time to cool down. "Just keeping you honest. You'd do the same for me."

Jim exhaled audibly. "Okay, you proved your point. Satisfied?" He looked around the room at the dark wood booths and the one small window. "This room needs more light. It's depressing."

Jim nodded to the pleasant young woman who was waiting on their table. "Another glass of what passes for wine here, please."

Pat was appalled. "Jim!"

Jim apologized to the young woman. "Don't mind me, I'm a curmudgeon."

The young woman shrugged over her shoulder. "No joke. I don't know how anybody can drink the wine here. Be right back."

*

When Jim was stuck in his thinking, a change of location often unstuck him. "Vermont for the weekend?" he suggested to Pat.

They drove up the Friday after Jim vented his frustration in the Wink and Nod. His mind wandered driving across Massachusetts but snapped to attention once they crossed the Vermont border. They stopped for lunch in Brattleboro, eating at a pub by the river, near the train station. Out of the blue, Jim said, "Julie Fisher."

Pat put down her veggie burger. "Excuse me?"

"Spinner's daughter, the one who lives in Vermont."

"Okay." Pat inflected the word like a question.

"In the mood for a visit to Dorset?"

7

The drive across Vermont to Dorset where Julie Fisher lived was twice as nice as the drive across Massachusetts: the roads less traveled, the rushing streams and mountain valleys more picturesque. Sorry, Massachusetts; I love ya, but you're no Vermont.

Julie Fisher welcomed Jim into her living room. "Your wife isn't with you this time?"

"No, Pat stayed back at the house. And we're not married, just living in sin."

"Sit down, won't you? Tea? Coffee?"

"Coffee, black, would be appreciated."

She returned in a minute with the coffee. He remembered her from their first meeting: trim, early forties, casual clothes, formal manners. She perched on the sofa, teacup on her knees.

"On the phone, you said you were trying to learn what happened to Dad's money. My husband, Jake, who's a financial advisor, says that Dad took bigger and bigger gambles as his fortune dwindled, which led to some big investors bailing out, which caused Dad to take even bigger risks. Jake cautioned that Dad didn't exhibit extraordinary financial acumen even at the beginning of his investment career – he rode the wave that everyone else was riding. Luck more than skill, was how Jake explained Dad's fortune."

"Your husband doesn't know of anything shady that might have precipitated your father's financial fall? Any fraud, any theft, any Ponzi scheme?"

"No, but it wouldn't surprise either of us to learn Dad cut corners and shaded the truth in order to keep up appearances. Dad took enormous pride in being accepted by the anointed. Anything that dented that image drove him insane. If I had to pick, I'd say being accepted by the class of people he aspired to join mattered more to Dad than money."

"Tell me more about his upbringing."

"Raised in Main Line Philadelphia by a father who made his money in railroads, and a mother who grew up on the wrong side of the tracks. My mother had impeccable manners, but she didn't come by them naturally and every so often Dad would make a snide comment about her lack of class. I always thought – in spite of or because of her working class background – that she had more class than Dad."

"You didn't like your dad much, apparently."

"Why do you say that? I found him difficult, but I respected him. He did a lot of good for others, was kind to waiters and taxi drivers, he just wasn't nice with Mother."

"The trial left unclear why an assistant pastry chef would kill your father."

"You tell me, Judge Randall. You presided at the trial."

"The prosecutor said in his closing statement that Max Ryan held a personal grudge against your father, that the motive wasn't financial. Some kind of slight your father committed against Ryan, some insult, some threat. Yet what you just said about your father makes me doubt that Max Ryan was the kind of man your father would insult."

Julie nodded. "I have a hard time imagining it."

"So somebody put Ryan up to killing your father."

"Or maybe he wasn't the killer." Julie leaned back on the sofa. "Dad's murder was so horrifying I locked the door on it for the longest time, but your visit unlocked the door. If an innocent man served time, that would make Dad's death even more horrifying."

She put her cup on the end table.

"Would you speak up for Max Ryan at his parole hearing?" Jim asked.

"I'm not at that point yet. If you find more evidence that points to a mistake, then, yes, certainly I would." She stood. "Let me show you something. Are you willing to take a short drive?"

He followed her to her car. The day was warm with a touch of dampness in the air. Her house was sheltered by trees, but a few steps beyond the house there was a clear view of a camelback mountain. Today the horizon of the mountain was a smudged pastel gray.

"Where are we going?" Jim asked as she began to drive.

"Have you ever seen a slate mine?"

"No."

"Well, you will now."

She turned left onto a steep road over a mountaintop to the town of Rupert where she turned right onto a gently curving road that led past corn fields and forested hills to the even smaller town of West Pawlet, and beyond it to a towering pile of sledge by the side of the road. "We're now in Slate Valley. This area north to Poultney was the colored slate capital of the world a century ago. Slate artisans from Italy and other countries settled here, raised their families here. But the demand for slate wore off as less expensive and lighter roofing material came on the market, and the slate industry dwindled to a few companies that still mine slate in the region. The debris from the early mines formed the ugly black mountains that stand sentry in this part of the country."

She pulled off the road beside a towering black pile of ugly, discarded slate. Below the pile was the pit from which the "good" slate had been mined. The pit was half-full of rainwater.

Julie Fisher turned in the driver's seat to face Jim. "Max Ryan didn't kill my father, did he, Judge Randall?"

"I have an uneasy feeling about it, that's all I can say at the moment."

"You must feel very uneasy or you wouldn't be pursuing this. You don't seem like a frivolous man."

"I hope not."

"What about the head chef? I never liked him. Could he have done it?"

"Olaf Anders was questioned by the police but was never a suspect."

"Why not?"

"They found no evidence that he had anything to do with the murder."

"I was young and didn't know Olaf well, but there was something about him that made me uncomfortable."

She turned the car around and headed back the way she came. They drove past a farm that made goat cheese and past dirt roads that disappeared into the forest. "Some injustices can't be corrected, can they?" She sounded as if she were asking herself. "Some wrongs can't be righted. Why is that?"

"I don't know," Jim replied, quietly.

She seemed startled to hear Jim's voice. She drove a little farther, then gave her head a shake. "How many of us would choose to be born if we could see what was coming?"

"Most, I believe."

"You do? I don't. But I love my husband, and I don't want to die, so I suppose I'll go on."

*

He and Pat ate that night at the white table cloth inn, and Jim ordered a Chinon red.

"Have you ever seen the Slate Valley?" he asked Pat.

"I didn't know there was a Slate Valley."

"In the western part of the state, straddling the New York border. Colored slate from there was prized by the rest of the world. I saw the debris, piles of broken slate beside the road."

Pat waited. She knew Jim wasn't talking about slate.

"The flaw in human reasoning is to think it mirrors the real world."

Pat continued to wait. Jim seemed lost in his own thinking.

"This is about the Ryan case, isn't it?" she finally prompted.

"Yes. I've seen cases where the preliminary evidence becomes accepted as conclusive, for example where a man with poison residue on his clothes is assumed to be the criminal. But what if all the assumption reveals is a lack of imagination? Do you follow?"

Pat nodded. "No, I don't. Are you saying Spinner wasn't poisoned?"

"No, that's not what I'm saying. I'm saying maybe there's an alternative explanation for how the arsenic residue got on Max Ryan's clothes. Maybe the real killer wanted to implicate Ryan in order to divert suspicion away from himself. Maybe straight-line thinking doesn't work in this case. Maybe the answer lies at the end of a dirt road half-hidden in the woods."

Pat stared at Jim. "My straight-line thinking tells me you have had too much wine."

When they got back to their house, Pat went to the bedroom to read in bed while Jim stood looking out the living room window. The sky over the Connecticut River Valley was a soft black, not harsh as in winter. Jim let his mind wander. He pictured Max Ryan languishing in a prison cell while he, Jim Randall, enjoyed being in a place he loved with the woman he loved. What was he failing to see? What clue had he overlooked?

They drove home the next day. As they neared Cambridge, Jim asked, "Who do we know in the restaurant business?"

"The only person who comes to mind is Bruce."

Bruce, co-owner and maître d' of Duck, Duck, Goose. He happily agreed to sit down with them before the daily meeting of his staff.

Bruce, when he was not greeting patrons at the front desk or patrolling the floor with a stack of menus, was a disconcerting sight, in motion even when sitting down. He drummed his fingers and jiggled his foot as the three of them spoke.

Jim explained his question and why he was asking it. How could someone who worked in a restaurant poison a patron and get away with it?

"Is the patron a regular customer?" Bruce asked.

"Yes."

"Does he have any food allergies? We know the food allergies of all our regulars and list them in our data base. Peanut allergies, to take one example, can be deadly for some people."

"Couldn't death by peanut be detected?"

"If the medical examiner finds poison, he or she may not look further."

"Could a restaurant worker murder someone with something as common as peanuts?"

"It's theoretically possible, but most people with serious food allergies carry syringes of epinephrine in case they go into anaphylactic shock."

"But it's possible?"

"Yes."

As they walked home from the restaurant, Pat was skeptical. "Why would someone resort to putting arsenic on Max Ryan's clothes if a food allergy was the actual cause of death?"

"To set Max Ryan up to take the rap."

"I'm confused. Didn't Michael Spinner die of arsenic poisoning?"

"Yes, but my recollection is that the medical examiner quickly came to that conclusion after arsenic was found on Ryan's clothes. Maybe the medical examiner reasoned backwards from the forensic findings."

"Seems improbable."

"Maybe, but if that's what happened, it worked. Max Ryan went to prison and whoever planned the whole thing has remained free."

Pat thought that over. "Nice try, Jim, but I wouldn't put money on it."

"Okay, it's a long shot. But I'm trying to jar my mind loose from the reasoning I used during Max Ryan's trial."

They continued walking. To walk home from Duck, Duck, Goose in daylight instead of darkness seemed an unnatural act. Jim grew frustrated as he walked. "Look, there's got to be an explanation other than what came out in the trial, I feel it in my gut. Something no one has thought of."

"Could Spinner have been poisoned before he got to the restaurant?" Pat asked.

"Or after, presumably. But that begs the question of the arsenic residue on Max Ryan's clothes." Jim dug in his pocket for his keys. At night he often picked the wrong key, but now in daylight he used the right key on the first try.

*

Time to check in with Ted Conover again. They met for a quick lunch near the courthouse. Ted was in the middle of a trial for arson.

Lunch counters near courthouses have a patina of gladiator, as lawyers joust for sandwiches and mentally prepare for the afternoon's battles.

"Still torturing yourself about the Ryan parole hearing?" Ted asked Jim, their words kept private by the noise around them.

"You know me well. Yes, I'm still considering whether to support his parole. I've met with Spinner's second wife, Roberta; his fiancée Pamela; one of his daughters, Julie; Max Ryan's wife, and Ryan himself."

"You've been busy."

"Give me my robe and my gavel so I can return to the stately pace of a trial."

"What's your conclusion? The guy was shafted, or justice was done?"

"No conclusion but a stronger than ever gut feeling that Ryan should not have received twenty-five years to life, and maybe should have been exonerated. If I had been a more experienced judge, I would have been more skeptical of some of the evidence. For example, I would have questioned assumptions such as that the poison that killed Skinner was in his Meyer lemon semifreddo, an assumption made because of the arsenic traces found on the clothes of Max Ryan, the man who prepared the dessert. But there wasn't proof since uneaten food is disposed of."

"Jim, you know as well as I that every case has unanswered questions, and I know that when your mind latches onto unanswered questions, you become a bloodhound. I admire that about you, but don't risk your reputation by speaking on Ryan's behalf unless you're pretty damn sure. You left the bench with no smudges on your reputation, don't make yourself look bad now."

Jim considered what Ted had said: my reputation matters enormously to me, but how can I let Ryan remain in prison if I made a mistake sending him there? Even a man with an ego as big as mine doesn't consider his reputation more important than another man's freedom.

He listened momentarily to the buzz in the lunch counter – talk of motions granted and denied, inpatient judges, and lying witnesses – so different than the somnolent, academic/arty atmosphere of The Long Gone. Normally he liked places where people grapple with real world problems, but justice was so fragile and the people who administer it so fallible that places like The Long Gone – where people withdraw from the world and dwell in their minds – may at times be preferable.

"I should leave it be, you're saying."

"No, if you have something to offer the parole board other than gut feeling or old judge regret, by all means speak up. Otherwise let the parole board do its thing."

Jim bristled a little at the "old judge" remark, but one of the reasons he had stayed friends with Ted after leaving the bench was that he could always count on Ted telling him what he thought, unfiltered. Come to think of it, Ted had inflected "old judge regret" wryly; I shouldn't have bristled at all.

Ted had to get back to court. Jim hung around the courthouse awhile, then headed home. He chose to walk the back streets near the courthouse – which he liked – then cut over to Cambridge Street in time to walk by the many hair, skin, and nail salons of Beauty Shop Row. This stretch of Cambridge Street in East Cambridge was his favorite part of the city. The variety of storefronts never lost the capacity to surprise, no matter how many times he walked the street.

He crossed the street at the live poultry shop, thought his way through familiar Inman Square, and reached home a little out of breath, but – hey – give a guy a break; I'm sixty-eight!

Pat had chosen to spend the night at her place. They spent nights alone only once in a while now, but doing so occasionally seemed to refresh their relationship.

He texted her: "Is there anything in the fridge I can heat up for dinner?"

Her reply: "Why don't you open the door of the fridge and look?"

He grumbled at that but did as he was told. There was some leftover chicken from last night. He would have that. But it was too soon for dinner, so he climbed upstairs – his breath back to normal – and picked a book to read: a Sophocles play he hadn't read, *Philoktetes*.

Soon he was as deep in the play as he was in his easy chair, and it startled him when his phone rang. He hated to be startled and answered with a growl, "Yeah."

A woman's voice, young. "Judge Randall?"

He tried to be civil. "Yes. Who is this?"

"Julie Fisher. Am I interrupting?"

He pulled himself upright in his chair. "Not at all. Forgive me for barking. I was half-asleep."

"I'm sorry, I can call back."

"No, no. Go ahead."

"Dad ate at the Fish and Fowl the night he died, is that correct?"

"Yes."

"Last night I remembered Dad saying that Teddy Demarco, the owner, was trying to sell the restaurant. Dad sounded upset because he ate there so often. Could that mean anything?"

"I don't know, but it's interesting. Did he say anything else?"

"Well, he said he might be forced to buy it himself, to keep it open. I couldn't tell if he was serious or sarcastic. He sort of threw the comment out, then dismissed it with the back of his hand as soon as he said it."

"Do you remember when he said this?"

"I've been trying to remember. Maybe six months before he died. I can't be sure of the timing."

"Do you know if he followed through on the idea?"

"If he did, he didn't tell me. He didn't buy the restaurant before he died, that much I know. I can't state whether he pursued the idea."

"This is helpful, Julie. Very helpful."

"I hope Max Ryan has not spent twenty years in prison for something he didn't do. I truly hope so. The more I think about it, the more it devastates me."

"I know the feeling. If you think of anything more, please don't hesitate to tell me."

He hung up, thought for a few minutes, then called Pat.

"Leftover chicken," she said before he could talk. "There's some in the fridge from last night."

"As I found out when I followed your helpful suggestion and opened the refrigerator door. But that's not why I'm calling. Julie Fisher just told me that her dad spoke about buying the Fish and Fowl. Julie couldn't tell if he was serious or not. Interesting, no?"

"That *is* interesting."

"The owner, Teddy Demarco, apparently wanted to sell, and Spinner was distraught at the thought of losing his favorite place to eat. How about that? Speaking of which, I shall now descend to the kitchen and heat up some leftover chicken. Here's an idea: I could open a restaurant serving nothing but micro-waved leftovers. I'd call it Leftovers. Catchy, don't you think?"

"The name alone would draw a crowd."

"Leftovers − short and fast for the Twitter Age. Why didn't I think of this before?"

"You should have been an entrepreneur."

"That's what I'm saying."

"Call me after dinner. I want to know how the chicken was."

"I may not be able to call. Food poisoning, you know."

She groaned. "You're lucky we're apart tonight. I have been known to do bodily harm."

He debated what wine would go with the leftover chicken and opened a bottle of inexpensive Cotés du Rhone, which goes with everything. He liked the wine better than the chicken. He drank his usual two glasses, so couldn't figure out why he felt unusually mellow after dinner. He climbed the stairs to his study (living in a townhouse was like living in a StairMaster), and finished the Sophocles play. Still no idea why he felt lighter of heart than in a while. Could that be a little noted effect of food poisoning? The answer to why didn't hit him until he went to bed and turned out the light.

He sat upright and switched on the light. Of course! Teddy Demarco. Where was he? Was he still alive?

8

Teddy Demarco sounded like the name of a made man, but when Jim googled him, he learned that Demarco was a pillar of Malden, the middle-income community where Demarco grew up and still lived. No blemishes on his record, nothing but good deeds – funding parks, building a feeder clinic for Boston's Deaconess Hospital, sponsoring boys and girls sports teams. He lived in an assisted living facility run by his local parish.

"Thanks for agreeing to see me," Jim said when he arrived at the hospital-like complex. Demarco met him in a common room full of card tables, potted plants, and recliners with electric lifts for people who had difficulty getting out of chairs. The windows looked out on a oblong courtyard.

Demarco was a small, bald man who had a gray aura. You could tell he had once been a very proud man, but time had withered him down to humble. Jim explained why he was there.

"The trial was a long time ago," Demarco said, encapsulated in an easy chair. "I can't remember much from back then. I barely remember what I ate for breakfast this morning."

"Michael Spinner was a frequent guest in your restaurant, wasn't he? Do you remember that?"

"Of course I do. I'm not senile. How old are you?"

"Sixty-eight."

Demarco gave a derisive puff of air. "I'm only twelve years older than you. Watch your step."

"Michael Spinner's daughter has told me that you wanted to sell Fish and Fowl, and that her father was unhappy about it. Any truth to that?"

"I don't remember names, I don't remember dates, but I remember business deals. No, I didn't want to sell the restaurant, I wanted to buy it from the landlord who raised our rent once too often to suit me. Olaf Anders, the chef of the Fish and Fowl, wanted in on the deal."

"What went wrong?"

Demarco's thin shoulders shrugged. "We couldn't raise the money. That's where Spinner came in. He was distressed at the thought of Olaf and me no longer running the restaurant, so he offered to back us financially."

"What happened?"

"The deal fell through. We made an offer to the landlord, which was accepted, then Spinner's financial guarantees proved worthless."

"The restaurant is still in business, isn't it?"

Demarco scowled. "For now. A national chain bought the property and has plans to turn it into a steakhouse. It's still the Fish and Fowl, but I wouldn't eat there to save my life."

"Do you remember the night Spinner died?"

"Not well. He didn't die at the restaurant. If he had, I would've remembered."

"He ate his favorite dessert that night."

"Meyer lemon semifreddo. That I remember. I remember the favorite foods of regulars. I remember the names of their children. I remember everything about running a restaurant."

"I understand your assistant pastry chef Max Ryan had standing orders to prepare it for Spinner every time he came in."

"That's right."

"And that Spinner died from eating it."

"That I wouldn't know."

"It was in the coroner's report."

"If you say so." Demarco seemed tired. "Are we almost done?"

"Just about. What happened to Olaf Anders, your chef? Where is he now?"

Demarco shrugged. "I fired him. He had a bad drug habit. He covered it up by coming down hard on the kitchen staff. After Michael Spinner died, fingers were being pointed in every direction, and that's when I got wind of Olaf's habit. I heard rumors that he surfaced later in San Francisco, but I don't know where he is now, or if he's alive. I'm tired. You'll have to leave now."

"Of course. Thanks for your time."

Jim walked to the Orange Line afterwards, thinking about what he had learned. Olaf Anders was the next person he wished he could talk to, although he couldn't think of a reason Anders would want to kill Michael Spinner. But then, Max Ryan had no obvious reason to kill him either.

That was the problem with this case. No person, known or otherwise, had any obvious reason to kill Spinner. And what person, known or otherwise, would choose Meyer lemon semifreddo as a murder weapon? Miss Scarlet in the study with the Meyer lemon semifreddo.

He paused as he neared the subway station to remind himself that his sole purpose in revisiting this case was to decide whether to support Max Ryan's petition for parole. Satisfy his conscience, not his curiosity. Right a wrong if there was a wrong. He did not have to prove who killed Spinner.

*

He stayed at Pat's that night, and they ate at a venerable Italian restaurant half-hidden amidst a cluster of office buildings.

"I visited Teddy Demarco in Malden today. Strange what he remembered and what he didn't. Do you know how long it's been since I've seen Malden?"

"A long time, I take it."

"A little forlorn but so much character. I forget what the small cities crowding Boston are like."

"Did you learn what you hoped to learn?"

"And then some. Demarco wanted to buy the restaurant from the landlord, Chef Anders wanted in on the deal, and Michael Spinner was going to advance the money but didn't come through. The landlord eventually sold the Fish and Fowl to a restaurant chain, which broke Demarco's heart. That gives him a plausible motive for killing Spinner, but it's hard for me to see how Demarco who wasn't a presence in the kitchen could have poisoned the semifreddo without Max Ryan knowing. On the other hand, Olaf Anders could conceivably have slipped poison in."

"Jim, what if you end with no clear idea of who murdered Spinner? Would you support Max Ryan's parole anyway?"

"I don't know."

"You might want to start considering that."

"I'm not ready to give up yet."

"Of course not." She looked across the table at him with a steady gaze, her eyes bright.

"You're giving me the look that says you know what I'm going to do before I do."

"No, I'm thinking how handsome you are."

He came close to blushing, a rarity. He parried with bluster. "Who can blame you?"

She leaned back in her chair. "Are you going to eat, or are you going to preen?"

"Can't I do both?"

They walked to her apartment afterward, the steep streets of Beacon Hill mostly deserted. The brick sidewalks echoed their footsteps.

"In answer to your question, if I can't come closer to proving Max Ryan's innocence, I'll leave his fate up to the parole board. In my experience, they do a pretty good job. They don't need a retired judge meddling based on nothing more than a hunch."

*

He enlisted Ernie Farrell and Sasha Cohen's help in finding what was known about the post-Fish and Fowl career of Olaf Anders. Apparently Anders relocated to San Francisco after DeMarco fired him and became a sous-chef at a locavore restaurant on the wharf. He stayed there for three years, then dropped out of sight.

"He was just gaining attention in San Francisco when he vanished," Sasha reported. "Very strange. I checked the obits, but his name didn't surface."

"Maybe nobody would hire him after word of his drug habit spread widely. Or he may be cooking under an assumed name in some out-of-the-way city."

"Any police reports on him?" Jim asked Ernie.

"None that I could find."

Jim wondered if Max Ryan knew where Anders was. He very much doubted it, but it was worth a try. He drove to the prison, endured the search, and waited for Ryan. Bleak was the name of the game in the visitors room.

Again, Ryan looked older than his years when he shuffled in. The difference this time was the hopeful look in his eyes.

"If you're hoping I have encouraging news, I'm sorry to disappoint you. I came because I have more questions."

Ryan sat down. "I guess I'm not surprised."

Jim again was struck by his soft, rounded voice. Jim sought a bad guy, but Ryan didn't oblige.

"I've talked to a bunch more people about your case. One of them was Teddy Demarco."

Ryan perked up. "You talked to Teddy?"

"You called him Teddy?"

"Everyone at the restaurant did. He was a demanding boss, but he treated people well. Did he tell you anything useful?"

"Not really. He knows little about what happened that night, other than that Michael Spinner had eaten there."

"That doesn't surprise me. Teddy didn't interfere with the daily operation of the restaurant. That was Olaf's baby."

"Tell me more about Olaf. What kind of a person was he?"

Ryan looked rattled. He glanced from side-to-side as if to see if anyone was listening. "Excellent chef, terrible human being. In contrast to how Teddy treated his staff, Olaf treated us like cattle."

"Do you know where he is now?"

Ryan looked at Jim as if he were crazy. "Do you see where I am? I'm in prison and have been for twenty years. How the hell would I know where he is?"

"I assume you talk to people on the outside."

"Except for my wife, not often."

"Then you don't know where he is?"

"He worked in San Francisco after leaving Boston, that much I know."

"But after that?"

"No idea."

"You told me that you prepared the semifreddo for Spinner that night."

"We already talked about this."

"Go over it again, maybe you'll remember something new. Did anybody help you with the preparation, even a little?"

"No, just me."

"Olaf Anders had nothing to do with it?"

"Nothing."

"Could he have slipped something into it without you knowing?"

Ryan shrugged. "I don't remember Olaf coming anywhere near my station that night. It's possible I turned my back at some point, but I doubt it." He shrugged again.

"Olaf and Demarco wanted to buy the Fish and Fowl from the landlord, and Spinner agreed to put up the money, but the deal fell through. Do you know anything about that?" Jim asked.

"We knew nothing. We were slaves and targets. Olaf would throw things at us. Luckily, his aim was as bad as his temper, but he would never share information like that with us. Wait, I just remembered something. After I finished plating Mr. Spinner's semifreddo, Teddy asked me to take the dessert to Mr. Spinner personally."

"Demarco personally asked you?"

"Yes, he appeared in the kitchen and came over to me."

"Did you do as he asked?"

"Of course, I was honored. I took the semifreddo to Mr. Spinner. He grasped my hand in both of his, shook it heartily, and thanked me for preparing his favorite dessert for so many years."

"Had he ever thanked you before?"

"Never. I never talked to him before. I never came into the dining room while customers were eating."

"Did he say anything else?"

"That he was grateful for the pleasure I had given him over the years. He was very emotional. I actually thought he might cry. Pamela Martin was with him. She smiled at me but said nothing."

"This is very helpful."

"Really? I didn't tell you anything."

"Yes, you did. You told me a lot."

*

At Jim's townhouse that evening he explained his thinking to Pat. "Any time a person deviates from a long-standing routine, it's potentially significant. Spinner had never asked to speak to Max Ryan before, never shaken his hand, never thanked him."

"What do you think it means?" They were eating at the kitchen table, with the angular three-deckers out the window.

"That he was saying goodbye to the restaurant."

"He had a premonition of death?"

"Maybe, but my guess is he was planning to get out of town. Thank about it. Spinner's hedge funds had lost so much of their value that he couldn't finance a deal to keep his favorite restaurant from being sold to a chain. He must have had angry investors breathing down his neck. His lifestyle was threatened, his reputation on the verge of ruin. Think of the humiliation of it all, not to mention the fear."

Pat got a bemused look on her face.

It annoyed Jim. "Why the look?"

"Sorry. I was thinking, now that my memoir is complete, I should write the Deadly Dessert Mysteries: Death By Semifreddo; Death By Chocolate Mousse. I see a TV series."

Pat expected a comeback. Instead, Jim's eyes grew distant.

"Where did your mind suddenly go?" Pat asked.

"Just considering other possible explanations for Spinner's display of emotion his last night. Maybe he had a terminal disease. Maybe he knew he was dying."

"Maybe he planned to take his own life," Pat said.

"He doesn't seem that type of man to me. Maybe he and Ryan had some sort of feud going on, as farfetched as that sounds. Remember: Pamela Martin and Max Ryan knew each other from Southie. Maybe they *had* been lovers in high school. Maybe they had taken up with each other again at the time of Spinner's death."

Pat's plate was empty. Jim had barely touched his food.

"Your reasoning is getting worrisomely byzantine," Pat said.

"What's byzantine about it? Sex seems like a straightforward motive to me."

"By your reasoning, Ryan should be dead, not Spinner." She stood and carried her plate to the sink. "Your turn to clean."

"But we ate takeout. No cleanup, remember?"

"Exhibit A. A pot in the sink."

"What on earth did you use it for?"

"Food."

Jim dumped most of his dinner down the disposal. "I think I'll pay Teddy DeMarco and Pamela Martin another visit."

9

Jim emerged from the Orange Line at Malden Center, pleased to be above ground after the subway. Malden's compactness and age lent it an atmosphere Jim liked. He stood for a minute getting his bearings, then headed towards the assisted living facility to see Teddy Demarco.

Jim had called ahead, and Demarco was waiting for him in the common room. "I knew you'd be back, but I didn't think it would be so soon."

"I have more questions."

Demarco looked neater, more put-together than last time; he had combed his unruly hair, thin though it was, and was dressed for a visitor. "I'm not surprised."

"I talked to Max Ryan again, and he told me something very interesting. He said you asked him to take Michael Spinner's dessert to him personally that night, something you had never done before."

"That's right. As I made my rounds in the diningroom, asking how everything was, chatting up the regulars like Spinner, he asked to speak to the man who had prepared his Meyer lemon semifreddo for so many years. I went into the kitchen and relayed the request to Max."

"Did Spinner say why he wanted to see Max?"

"He wanted to thank him."

"Did he indicate why that night, of all nights?"

"No, he didn't. And I didn't ask."

"He was with his fiancée, I understand."

"Pamela Martin. Yes, she often dined with him. Very nice young woman."

"Were you surprised by their engagement?"

"Why would I be surprised?"

"Because of the age gap."

Demarco considered that. "It wasn't that large a gap. Besides, they seemed to like each other, that was enough for me."

"Anything else unusual about that night? Anything odd? Spinner's mood, perhaps?"

"Come to think of it, he did seem different that night."

"How so?"

"He usually kept the staff at a distance, but that night he seemed highly emotional. Wistful. Weepy."

"He didn't indicate why?"

"No, why would he? It was none of my business."

"Thank you. This has been very helpful."

"I don't get many visitors. Come whenever you like. If I run out of memories, I'll make some up."

Jim had a long wait at the subway station, long enough to replay what he had learned. Something made Spinner emotional that night at the Fish and Fowl. Something made him ask to see Max Ryan.

Jim gritted his teeth as the Orange Line train – worn and dirty as a discarded pair of running shoes – pulled into Downtown Crossing station. Because of a twenty minute delay the car was packed. Squeezed by a swaying scrum of humanity, Jim clung to the overhead railing, thoughts of Max Ryan's parole hearing shoved from his head. He had to change trains which he usually hated but today was grateful for...until he had to wait twelve minutes for the

Red Line to Harvard Square, only to find it just as crowded as the Orange Line.

When he came up for air, never had the Out of Town newsstand looked as good. Even the Pit surrounding the T stop, where young druggies and dropouts hung and strummed their out-of-tune guitars, looked almost folksy instead of menacing.

He walked the few blocks to his townhouse, full of bile. Maybe he should move in with Pat. Live on orderly Beacon Hill. Avoid the crass commercialism and heartbreaking homelessness of Harvard Square. Which begged the question, would Pat have him? She liked her privacy as much as he did. Their living arrangement suited them both, had served them well since they became a couple.

Idle thoughts, discarded as soon as he unlocked his door and entered the safety of his house.

He called her soon after he arrived.

"How did it go with Demarco?" Pat asked. Jim liked her voice. There was a declarative quality to it even when she asked a question, but he was grouchy from the subway.

"Have you ever heard me complain about our antiquated subway system?" he asked.

"Many times. *Many* times."

"Once more. Our system sucks, it stinks, its insulting."

"Are you done?"

"How come our country can do apps but can't do subways?"

"Demarco?"

"The meeting went well. He's glad for company. He confirmed that Michael Spinner asked to speak with Max

Ryan. When I asked Demarco if Spinner seemed different that evening, he said he sounded wistful, nostalgic."

"As if he were saying goodbye?"

"Which leads me to think he knew what was coming."

"But how?"

"Someone threatened him, and I'm thinking it was Max Ryan. That when Spinner asked to speak to Ryan, it wasn't to thank him, it was to say, I'm not afraid of you."

"To head him off. To tell him, in effect, I'm on to you."

"Yes," Jim said. "But even if we're right, we still don't know why Ryan would want to kill Spinner."

"Didn't you say that Max Ryan and Pamela Martin were friends in high school? Isn't it possible that Max wanted to take up with Pamela but she spurned him in favor of Spinner?"

"That could be. Maybe Pamela will tell me."

They again met at The Long Gone. Again Jim got the impression of an attractive woman in her forties who paid more attention to her thoughts than her appearance.

"How's John?"

"You remembered my husband's name."

"A judge never forgets."

Another impression: Pamela didn't readily smile or frown. Her mind was lively, but her face was not a billboard. An internal person, a self-contained person. If Spinner had survived and he and Pamela been married as planned, Pamela would not have been the typical trophy wife.

"What more have you learned, Judge? Did Max Ryan kill my fiancé?"

"I still don't know. I wish I did. Here's what I have learned. Your fiancé asked to see Ryan in order to thank him for preparing Meyer lemon semifreddo every time he ate at the Fish and Fowl. Do you remember him doing that?"

"Yes, I do."

"You hadn't mentioned that before."

"I didn't think it was important."

"Could you hear what your fiancé and Max Ryan said to each other when they spoke?"

"Clearly. I was sitting next to Michael."

"And?"

"Michael thanked him for all the years of making his favorite dessert. He looked very intense and shook Max Ryan's hand in both of his. It seemed unusually heartfelt for a self-assured man like Michael."

"How did Ryan respond?"

"He seemed humbled, unsure how to respond. I would bet this had never happened to him before, the assistant pastry chef summoned into the dining room to be thanked by a long-time patron."

"Did he say anything?"

"He mumbled thanks. I'm not sure of the exact words, something about being glad Michael appreciated his work."

"There was no hint of annoyance or irritation?"

"Why would there be?"

"If Michael's thanks contained a note of condescension or mocking."

"Far from it. Michael was as sincere as I'd ever seen him. There was none of the haughtiness he sometimes showed."

"Teddy Demarco, the owner at the time, used the words, 'nostalgic, wistful,' to describe your fiancé's mood that evening. Is that how you would describe it?"

"I think I understand what Demarco was referring to, but I wouldn't use those words. To me, Michael seemed relieved, not nostalgic. Michael had suffered several business setbacks in the months before and during dinner he told me that everything was going to work out fine. I took that as a sign that his funds were doing better, that things were looking up. He thanked me for believing in him. He teared up as he thanked me."

"I need to tell you that his funds had not improved, he was still in hot water."

"Then why would he seem upbeat?"

"I don't mean to challenge your recollection – you heard what you heard – but maybe your happiness with Michael colored your interpretation of his mood. My guess is that his business losses had humbled him, made him grateful for what he had, not necessarily that his work was on the upswing."

She frowned, for her a dramatic change of expression. "You may be right," she said. "I suppose that's possible. But why would Max Ryan want to kill Michael? I fail to understand."

"That's what I'm trying to discover. I apologize for the next question, but were you having any sort of romantic relationship with Ryan at the time of your fiancé's death?"

"No, I told you, we were friendly in high school. Period. We were never lovers."

"A flirtation your fiancé could have misinterpreted?"

A quarter-turn of her body and a deep sigh of agitation. "I told you. NO."

"I had to ask. I promise I won't give up looking. I know you want to do the right thing."

"Yes, I do." She clasped her hands together to control her anger.

"Are you okay? Would you like more coffee?"

"No, I'm fine," she said.

"Will you call me if anything else comes to mind about that night? I know I upset you, but will you do that?"

"I will." They stood. "Are we supposed to take our cups to the counter?" she asked.

"It's appreciated, but not essential."

She lifted her cup and dutifully carried it to the counter. Jim did likewise.

Outside The Long Gone, she said, "I guess I have more buried feelings about Michael's death than I realized, even after twenty years."

"Who could blame you?"

"Goodbye, Judge Randall." She extended her hand.

"Take care."

He walked partway to Pat's, past Beauty Shop Row and the money transfer storefronts, past the vest pocket stores stocking groceries from Brazil, Haiti, and Vietnam, past the Portuguese social club and the Martin Luther King branch library. His mind worked well on this route.

Demarco and Pamela Martin differed in their interpretation of Michael Spinner's mood on the evening of his death, but both had noticed something unusual. Wistful, nostalgic. Relieved, overflowing with gratitude. None of the above. His death could be coincidence –

stranger things have happened – but Jim would bet Spinner had a premonition of what was about to happen.

Pieces of the jigsaw puzzle fit together, but gaps remained. What was missing? Jim sat on a bench beside the library and tried to fill the gaps. Premonition, yes or no? Who and why? A lot was missing. Yet he felt he had made progress.

He sat on the bench a few more minutes, then stood, stiff knees and all, and walked the rest of the way to Beacon Hill, more confident than when he started.

He used his key to get in. "Hello?" Pat wasn't home.

He helped himself to wine and stretched out on the living room sofa. "Hi," his prone self said when Pat got home a short time later.

She jumped. "Don't scare me like that."

He swung his legs onto the floor. "I live here part-time, remember?"

She recovered quickly. "Remind me of your name?"

He stood and closed the gap between them. "George Clooney," he said, kissing her. It had never occurred to him until that moment that one among the many reasons he liked kissing her was he didn't have to lean down. His late wife, bless her soul, was a foot shorter than he.

She pulled away to get a good look at him, then kissed him back. "I thought I recognized you, George. There are so many men, you know."

"It must be hard to keep them all straight." He retrieved his wine glass from the floor by the sofa and took it into the kitchen.

"How was your meeting with Pamela Martin?" Pat called from the living room.

"Good. It went well. I'll tell you about it in a minute." He rinsed his glass and put it in the dishwasher. "I have a feeling I'm getting close."

She appeared in the doorway of the kitchen, brandishing a 9x12 spiral bound book. "The galleys of my memoir arrived today."

"Wow! What took you so long to tell me?"

"You were molesting me."

He crossed the room to her. "This is wonderful, Pat. I'm so proud of you."

"Don't tear up, you big baby. It could have been *our* memoir, remember?"

"And deprive you of the pleasure of gloating? I'm not that selfish."

"Will you glance at it?" she shyly said.

"Of course. But how does it look to you?"

"To be honest? It scares the crap out of me. This is real. People I don't know may read it. What will they think of me?"

He kissed her forehead and stepped away. "I've never known you to be self-conscious."

"I've never sent my words out into the world before."

"We have to celebrate. How?"

They settled on the narrow bistro at the base of the hill. He ordered champagne.

"To the author." He raised his glass.

She raised her glass. "I'm humbled by your applause. Thanks to the Academy, my parents, every schoolteacher I ever had from pre-school to law school, and most of all I'd like to thank my dear, beloved partner, Jim, who would be listed as co-author of the book if he had, in fact, written any of it." They clicked glasses and drank.

She was sitting with her back against the long window to Charles Street. The window chopped pedestrians off at the waist. Heads seemingly unattached to bodies streamed by, some alone, some in pairs, some in clusters.

Jim thought of Pamela Martin sitting in the dimly lit Long Gone, then looked at Pat silhouetted against the window onto brightly lit Charles Street. He thought of Max Ryan sitting in his prison cell – was it dimly or brightly lit? He thought of Michael Spinner emotionally pumping Max Ryan's hand and thanking him for the semifreddo over the years. "That's it!" Jim cried, startling Pat and the nearby diners.

She looked at him blankly, unsure what to make of his outburst. "What is?"

"The handshake!"

"Are we talking about Michael Spinner?"

"Yes. I know we're celebrating your galleys, but I just realized how the kitchen clothes Max Ryan wore than night could show traces of arsenic."

"Are you suggesting that the arsenic could have been passed from Spinner to Ryan by the handshake?"

"Why not?"

"Because why would Spinner have poison on his hands?"

"Or his clothes, maybe on his sleeves – remember, the handshake was hearty, a two-fisted pump. Maybe Spinner met with whoever poisoned him *before* coming to the restaurant. Maybe that person was a client, and maybe they shook hands."

They fell silent. The diners on either side had resumed their conversations as if Jim hadn't cried out. Jim gazed at Pat's head silhouetted against the window.

"Be right back," he told her. He walked outdoors to call Pamela Martin. It had turned chilly, and he shivered. A man answered.

"This is Jim Randall. Is Pamela Martin there?"

"Just a minute." The man covered the phone. "Pam! Phone call for you. Jim Randall."

She came on the phone quickly. "Is something wrong?"

"Not at all. I have one more question. Did Michael Spinner meet with anybody before the two of you went to the restaurant?"

"Not that I know of. He picked me up at my apartment and we went straight to the restaurant."

"According to the police report, he fell ill on the cab ride home, is that right?"

"Yes. By the time we arrived, Michael felt so terrible I had the taxi take us to the hospital."

"Thank you. This is very helpful."

"Judge, have you discovered something?"

"Nothing definite. I'm just wondering if the police and DA have ruled out all possible suspects. I'm wondering if your fiancé had been poisoned before he got to the restaurant. Arsenic acts quickly but not instantly."

"It horrifies me to think the wrong man may have spent twenty years in prison."

"Yes, but better to find out now than never."

*

Time to sit down with Ted Conover again. They met in his office. Cambridge Street traffic hummed outside.

"I have another question about Michael Spinner's murder."

"I guessed."

"Did Spinner meet with anybody in the hours just before he died?"

"Pamela Martin, of course, but we ruled her out as a suspect quickly. The only possible motive she had was the foundation Spinner set up for her to run in the event of his death, but she wouldn't inherit anything if he died before they were married."

"I meant anyone else, a friend, a business partner, a client. Did he meet with anybody before he picked Pamela Martin up to go to the restaurant?"

"No."

"Are you sure?"

"It is hard to be sure of a negative. But our office and the detectives working the case couldn't locate anyone who met with Spinner in the hours immediately before he and his fiancée went to the Fish and Fowl. What's the angle you're working?"

"That whoever poisoned Spinner did so before he got to the Fish and Fowl."

"We considered that and ruled it out for two reasons: one, we couldn't locate anyone, and two, poison residue was found on Max Ryan's clothes in the kitchen."

"And I know how this works. As soon as traces of arsenic were found on Max Ryan's clothes, the investigation narrowed. Am I correct?"

"Jim, why are you taking such an interest in this case? I take that back, I understand why. You're crazy."

Jim chuckled under his breath. "I prefer to think of myself as a crusader for justice. Did you know that Michael Spinner asked to see Max Ryan while he and his fiancé were eating dinner?"

"Asked to see him?"

"Yes, he asked Teddy Demarco, the restaurant owner, to have Max Ryan come into the dining room so he could thank Ryan for making his favorite dessert each time they ate there. According to Pamela Martin, Spinner gave Ryan a vigorous two-fisted handshake. It's conceivable that the arsenic was passed from Spinner to Ryan without either of them realizing it."

"Conceivable, but I'll stick with the theory presented when the case was tried in court, *your* court. That Ryan did it. Which raises a point – I've known you a long time, we were both young and handsome when we started..."

"I'm still handsome."

"...and I've known you to stand for the right thing more often than not, but sometimes I worry that your pride gives you tunnel vision."

"Do you think that's happening now?"

Ted spread his hands. "Ryan may be paroled this time anyway, and I hate to see a good judge ruin his reputation by admitting he blew his first murder trial."

"But that's precisely the reason I must pursue this, don't you understand?"

"Easy, Jim. I'm your friend."

Jim stood. He could see the Cambridge Street traffic through Ted's window. The scene was so familiar from all his years working in the nearby courthouse that he was momentarily disoriented as to time. "Sorry to bristle. I will think about what you said, Ted. You may be right. I may be pursuing this because I hate to admit I am wrong. Thank you as always for being honest with me."

Ted nodded. He came around the desk and patted Jim's shoulder. "You been working out? You look good."

Jim laughed. "Like hell."

He felt dispirited when he left Ted's office. He walked partway home, then caught the 69 bus the rest of the way. Pat was there, proofing the galleys in Jim's kitchen.

She looked up.

"Ted thinks I'm hurting my reputation."

Pat put down her pencil. "He said that?"

"In so many words. Do you think I am?"

"No, and I'm disappointed in Ted for saying that."

"He's a prosecutor. That's how he thinks. But he's fair. How do the galleys look?"

"A strange thing, I'm used to them now. The fear is gone."

He walked to the table and kissed her on the forehead.

"What brought that on?" Pat said in wonder.

"The sight of you reading your galleys."

"Jim Randall, I swear you are getting mushy."

10

Time was running out. Max Ryan's parole hearing was less than a month away. Jim met Sasha Cohen for lunch in the South End.

"Are newspapers going to survive?" he asked Sasha to avoid talking about his real subject.

"We still haven't figured out how to replace the lost revenue from classified ads. Everyone thought digital ads would do the trick, but they were wrong. Print is the only thing sustaining the business, yet it's not bringing in enough dough to fund news gathering at its previous level. The trend is to charge online readers for content, and that's working pretty well so far, at least for established news organizations."

"Like the *Globe*?"

"To an extent, yes. The *New York Times, Wall Street Journal, Financial Times*."

Jim had met Sasha when she wrote for an alternative weekly that had since gone out of business. Her face had gained a gravity it lacked before, but she still looked youthful enough to pass for a reporter for *Seventeen Magazine*.

Avoidance has a finite shelf-life. "I'm running out of time," Jim finally said. "Max Ryan's parole hearing is less than a month away. If my current theory doesn't pan out, I don't know where to turn."

"What's your current theory?"

"That Spinner was poisoned before he got to the restaurant. That the traces of arsenic found on Max Ryan's clothes got there when he shook hands with Michael Spinner."

Sasha chewed a mouthful of pasta. "Anything's possible, I guess."

"You don't sound convinced."

She leaned her elbows on the table. "I think the answer to who killed Michael Spinner is hidden in Spinner's money problems. His hedge fund was in deep trouble before he died. He had made a string of iffy investment decisions that lost big money and his fund was hemorrhaging investors. Hedge funds have built-in restrictions on when investors can pull out, so he wasn't in danger of a sudden and total collapse, but he must have been living in mortal terror of not being able to pay off his investors when they wanted out."

"Yet in the midst of this he got engaged to a young woman who is no dummy. Why would he take the chance of marrying again if he were in mortal terror of losing it all?" Jim countered.

"Love? Ego?"

Jim didn't slow down. "He even named Pamela head of a foundation to be set up after he died."

"A foundation that would probably have no money by the time he died if his hedge fund kept hemorrhaging at the same rate. I'll stick to love when it comes to women, and money as the motive for his murder."

Jim ordered espresso and Sasha a cappuccino; the espresso was bitter compared to The Long Gone's.

"Only one of our business writers was with the *Globe* twenty years ago, but he remembers the murder well. The poisoning of a hedge fund manager doesn't happen every day," Sasha said.

"Does he have any new insights?"

Sasha shook her head. "Not really. A lot of investors were angry at Spinner, but most of his clients were experienced investors, familiar with the ups and downs of the markets, not prone to violence. The one insight he shared was that by the time of Spinner's death, a rumor was spreading through the financial world that Spinner's hedge fund might be little more than a Ponzi scheme. Rumors like that can take on a life of their own and generate a dangerous amount of pent-up anger."

He said goodbye to Sasha on the sidewalk after lunch and walked in the direction of Back Bay Station and the Orange Line. His brain was too busy for his eyes to register what he was seeing.

He reached Back Bay Station but wasn't ready to brave the subway, so he kept walking.

What Sasha had said made sense, but Jim's thoughts kept returning to the handshake – something crucial about the handshake was eluding Jim. He wasn't viewing it from the correct perspective. Stretch your mind, he told himself. Whatever the answer, you'll wonder what took you so long to find it when you do.

He was surprised to find himself in the Public Garden. He had covered a lot of ground and was proud of his legs for not being tired.

He felt his imp coming on, which happened whenever he felt stuck in his sleuthing. When he felt impish, he liked to share it with Pat, since it took her a beat or two to realize he was kidding. Of course, she then gave as good as she got, better in fact, and when that happened he had to be on guard.

Now that he was near Beacon Hill, he detoured to her apartment instead of going home. His pause in the Garden to admire his leg strength had sapped him of energy, and by the time he climbed the hill to Pat's, he was breathing heavily.

His keys were buried beneath who knows what in his pocket, so he rang her doorbell. Her initial expression upon opening the door was surprise, followed by concern.

"Are you okay? I didn't expect you. Why did you ring the bell?"

"Too lazy to dig out my keys."

She stepped aside. "Cone in and sit down. I'll get you some water."

He sat on her sofa and caught his breath. When she appeared with a glass of water, he explained his presence. "I had lunch with Sasha Cohen, then walked back from the South End. I did okay until I started admiring my legs."

She sat down beside him and kept a straight face. "Why did you admire your legs?"

"I've got great legs, that's why. Everyone says so."

"I've heard that. Wouldn't know from personal experience." She rose from the sofa and crossed the room to the table. "I have work to do, but you know where the full-length mirror is if you want to admire your legs."

"Are you still working on that damn book?"

"Jealous?"

"Not with legs like mine."

*

The one person Jim hadn't been able to speak to was Olaf Anders, the head chef at the time Michael Spinner was poisoned. He had been questioned by the police and never implicated, but he might have useful knowledge without knowing it. Anders had cooked in San Francisco after the Fish and Fowl, but if he was still there or where he had gone was unknown to Jim .

With Ernie and Sasha's help, Jim was able to learn that Anders had abruptly fled San Francisco, turning up some years later in Paris. He was still there, cooking at the Jardin de Petits, a tiny bistro in the 7th arrondissement.

Pat spoke French well enough to call the restaurant and ask for Anders. He wasn't there when she first called, but on the second try, she reached him.

"Olaf Anders? Just a moment, please, I'm going to put Judge Randall on the phone." She handed the phone to Jim.

"Mr. Anders, I'm Jim Randall. Before I retired, I tried the murder case of Max Ryan, your assistant pastry chef at the Fish and Fowl. I'd like to ask you a few questions."

Anders spoke English with a barely perceptible Scandinavian accent. "That was a long time ago. Why are you interested?"

"He is up for parole, and I am rethinking his case."

A pause. "I have no wish to talk to you."

"I am not calling about you. My only interest is Max Ryan. He has been in prison for twenty years."

"It is evening here and we are very busy. I must go."

"May I call you later?"

"Bonne nuit, Judge."

Jim put down the phone and turned to Pat. "No luck."

"Given his drug history, I don't blame him."

"It was worth a shot."

"Let's take ourselves out to dinner this evening."

"I'm not in the mood. I wouldn't enjoy it."

"Maybe you'll change your mind."

"No, I won't."

"You're sure of that?"

"I am."

Full stop. Jim didn't know what to try or who else to call. He grew surly when stuck. Pat usually handled his grouch with good humor, but there was a limit to how indulgent she was willing to be. For which he was secretly grateful. He demanded the right to grumble but didn't want to get away with it indefinitely – knew himself well enough to glimpse when he was being unreasonable even if he refused to face it head on. "Know thyself," Socrates famously said; Judge Randall's reply, "But not too well."

He needed to spare Pat his bad mood. She hadn't led him to this dead end. "I've changed my mind. Let's eat out," he said as the time neared.

"Good idea," she said with a straight face.

"What's your next move?" she asked as they walked around the corner to Duck, Duck, Goose.

"I don't know, and don't keep asking me."

"That's the first time I've asked."

"You'll keep asking, I know."

"You know that for a fact?"

"Yes."

They were walking to Duck, Duck, Goose on a night when the sky was crowding Cambridge, as if there were no room for both city and sky. Bruce greeted them at the restaurant door.

He showed them to their usual table in the corner by the window, placed menus at their places and left them to bicker. Pat led the way: "No joke. I don't like it when you think you can read my mind."

"I wasn't serious."

"I know, but I still don't like it."

"But you *will* keep asking."

"How do you know?"

"Brilliance, thy name is Jim Randall."

Their waiter approached. "Good to see you again. May I start you off with sparkling water, still water, tap water?"

"Tap is fine," Pat replied.

"Let's have a bicker-free dinner," Jim said when the waiter had gone. "You won't give me a hard time, and I won't read your mind. At least not until we're walking home under portentous skies and I start to feel surly again."

She rolled her eyes.

They did have a bicker-free dinner, and neither of them spoke on the short walk home, content in each other's company. Jim was the first to speak. In the dark of his hallway, before he turned on the lights: "I hate to admit defeat, but I've run out of ideas. I don't know what to try."

"You've got a month until the parole hearing."

"Which will whiz by."

"You'll think of something. Don't give up."

*

So as not to feel completely defeated, Jim paid Max Ryan another visit. By now, the prison visitors room with its concrete and steel felt familiar. The hopeful look on Ryan's face broke Jim's heart.

"Do you have good news?" Ryan asked.

Jim shook his head. "I'm afraid not. Lots of blind alleys. Nothing probative. I'm sorry."

Ryan's face fell. To see a man who had so little hope to begin with lose the rest of his hope was terrible to see.

"I won't give up. I'll keep trying," Jim said quietly.

Ryan replied as quietly. "I know you will. This isn't your fault."

"There's a distinct possibility the parole board will grant you parole without my support. This is your second try, and you have a spotless prison record."

"But I still won't admit guilt. That's what they want me to do."

"I'll keep trying. Pat called Olaf Anders, but he wouldn't talk to her."

Ryan perked up a little. "Where is Olaf now? I heard his cocaine habit got the best of him and he lost his job in San Francisco."

"He's in Paris, working at a obscure bistro. How the mighty have fallen."

Ryan lowered his eyes. "I worry about my wife, Judge. I worry she'll leave me." Ryan became emotional.

"She's stuck with you this long."

"Yes, but if I'm not paroled this time, I don't know what she'll do."

"I can understand why you're worried, but I think she's devoted to you."

"She's the only reason I have for getting out of bed in the morning. You don't know what it's like waking up in a cell every day. You never get used to it, especially when you're innocent."

"I think she'll wait for you, and I repeat that you may be paroled even if I don't find new evidence."

Ryan wanly nodded.

Jim walked from the prison marveling how different the world seemed outside its walls. Scientists need look no further than prison to confirm the existence of parallel universes.

He walked to the visitors parking lot feeling terrible he hadn't been able to deliver better news to Ryan. The way Ryan reacted to Jim's discouraging report – defeated rather than angry, deflated rather than furious – convinced Jim that he truly believed he didn't belong in prison. Jim was more determined than ever to prove him right.

11

"I'll bet that Olaf Anders will talk to me if I show up in person."

Pat did a double take. "Go to Paris? Are you serious?"

"Why not? We enjoyed it when we went before." They had gone to Paris together shortly after the Ernie Farrell case.

"I think you just want an excuse to go again."

"That may be, but I can't stand defeat, and I think Olaf Anders may be my last hope. I have to try."

Given their last-minute booking, there were no aisle seats remaining on the plane, which meant Jim's knees became bonded to the seatback in front of him. When the cabin lights dimmed and the seatback in front of him fell like a toppled tree, his kneecaps whimpered in pain. He wanted to rub them but couldn't wedge his hands between kneecap and seatback. Pat, meanwhile, fell asleep as soon as dinner was cleared.

He had no hope of sleep. He watched two episodes of Law and Order, fighting the urge to yell "objection," did a crossword puzzle, went to the bathroom, sat back down and tried to sleep, again to no avail. Grumpy did not adequately describe his mood when the plane landed at Charles de Gaulle.

They stayed at the hotel in the Marais where they stayed before. The nineteen rooms were small but well appointed. The staff was friendly.

They didn't plan on a lengthy stay, so had packed lightly. They unpacked their bags and lay down for a quick nap.

He felt much better when he awoke. Pat was still napping, so he went to the window. Across the narrow street, his eyes skimmed the rooftops of Paris, no two alike.

"How long have you been up?" he heard Pat say.

"Not long." He turned to look at her. "Shall we get something to eat? I'm hungry."

"Let me wash up."

When she emerged from the bathroom, she said, "When are you embarking on your fool's errand?"

"Are you sure that's what it is?"

"I think you just wanted to be in Paris. Well, we're here."

"Patience. Wait and see."

They went around the corner to a café on rue de Rivoli and had tartines and a glass of Gigondas.

"Let's check out the Jardin de Petits," Jim said when they finished eating.

They had a hard time finding the bistro. It was located in a back alley in the 7th and was so unassuming as to be easy to miss. There was no sign of activity. Lettering on the door gave the hours as noon until midnight, Monday through Friday. It was Sunday.

"A place for office workers to have lunch and locals to eat dinner," Jim said, turning to Pat.

"You've got something on your mind, don't you? Something you're not telling me."

"Maybe. But I don't know what it is yet. I'm turning ideas over in my mind and I'll tell you when I know."

"Fair enough. Okay, we'll eat dinner here tomorrow. I'll call and make a reservation."

Pat made a reservation for vingt heure, late for them but early for Parisians. Jim was starving by the time eight arrived.

They walked in and were taken aback by the bistro's small size. There were six tables and three stools at a minuscule counter. Cozy would be one word to describe it, threadbare would be another. The man who worked the counter came to greet them at the door and didn't consult a list of reservations when Pat gave their name.

"I wonder if anyone besides us made reservations," Pat said when they were seated at a table near the door. The counterman propped the chalkboard menu against a chair back and wished them bon appétit.

They ate their poulet rôti and salade verte with impatience, speaking quietly because every word could be overheard by everyone in the bistro. "You speak French. The next time the waiter comes to our table, ask if we could speak with the chef," Jim said to Pat, which is what Pat did.

The waiter furrowed his brow. "Was something wrong with the food?".

"Mais, non. Au contraire. Tout c'est bon," Pat replied.

The waiter shrugged his shoulders and went into the kitchen. In a moment, a tall blonde man with a deeply-lined face emerged and walked to their table, wiping his hands on his apron.

In impeccable English with a barely perceptible accent he said, "You asked to see me?"

Jim spoke. "Are you Olaf Anders?"

The man took a step backward. "Who are you?"

"I spoke to you on the phone from the States. I'm Judge Jim Randall."

"I told you on the phone, I have nothing to say."

"You have nothing to fear. We're not here about you. We're here about Max Ryan."

"I don't understand why you are so interested in him."

"I told you over the phone. I was the judge in the trial that convicted him of murder. He is up for parole later this month and my conscience compels me to revisit the case."

"You come all this way because of your conscience?"

"Paris is a beautiful city. Isn't that reason enough?"

"I'm sorry. I can't help you. My luck has changed, as you can see, and I'm not inclined to help Max. If not for him, I wouldn't be cooking at this hole-in-the-wall."

The waiter came to their table and whispered in Olaf Anders's ear.

Anders stood. "I have to get back to the kitchen," he said to Jim and Pat.

"Wait, what do you mean, 'if not for him'?"

"You'll have to excuse me. Enjoy your visit to Paris." Anders strode to the kitchen without giving Jim time to say more.

Jim waited until he was gone, then turned to Pat. "That's what I thought. He was the anonymous caller to the DA's office who first pointed the finger at Max Ryan."

"To what purpose?"

"I'm guessing that Anders feared that Max would rat on him to Demarco about his drug habit and wanted to get Max out of the way."

"Why didn't you tell me this is what you were thinking? It would have explained your sudden urge to see Paris."

"Because it seemed far-fetched, even to me."

Jim signaled for the check. When it came, he jotted the name of their hotel on the back and handed it to the counterman. "Please give this to the chef," he said, which Pat repeated in French.

The man looked at the note and nodded.

The bistro was on a street so narrow and dark it became a hidden valley and the six-story buildings bracketing it mountain cliffs. Pat and Jim stood on the sidewalk outside the bistro and considered whether to stop at a café for a drink before going back to the hotel. While they talked, Jim glanced in the bistro window and saw the counterman rip the note with the name of their hotel into little pieces.

They walked through side streets so quiet it seemed impossible they were in a bustling city and emerged onto the wide Blvd St. Germain with its flowing river of cars. Hard to imagine it was in the same city as the silent streets they had just walked.

"If I'm right about Olaf Anders tipping off the DA's office to save his job, the irony is that he lost his job anyway. Getting Max Ryan arrested for murder didn't change the outcome for Olaf, only for Max. How about that drink before we go back?" Jim asked near the Metro.

"I'm for it."

They chose a sidewalk café a block off the boulevard. The outdoor heaters were on to cut the chill.

Pat ordered hot chocolate, Jim a cognac.

"Am I a complete idiot for pursuing such ephemeral leads?" Jim asked after the waiter brought their drinks.

"Not a complete idiot."

"At the start of my judicial career I probably gave the DA's office too much deference, I see that now, but even if I had been more skeptical at the time, the DA's office had good reason to zero in on Max as the prime suspect in Spinner's death: an anonymous caller who steered them towards Max, a fellow kitchen worker who thought he saw Max add something suspicious to Spinner's semifreddo, followed subsequently by the lab tests which discovered traces of arsenic on the clothes Max wore that night. I can see why they didn't pursue other explanations as thoroughly as they pursued Max. Knowing that makes me more comfortable about supporting his parole, if I do."

"How are you going to decide?"

"Make Olaf Anders's life miserable. He's the one who fled the country. He has more to hide." Jim raised his glass and cloaked his voice in judicial robes. "To whoever invented cognac."

Pat clicked glasses, "Whomever."

"'To whoever' as a prepositional form can be used as a subject."

"Who just finished proofing the galleys of her book?"

"Who is a grammar prig?"

Back in the hotel room, they undressed, got in bed, and fell asleep quickly, in spite of the time difference. Pat woke up early the next morning, Jim soon after. The first words out of his mouth: "Guess where we're going to eat lunch and dinner."

"Jim! The food's awful."

"What's more important, a good meal or breaking Olaf Anders's will?"

"That's a straight line if I've ever heard one."

"Let the record show the witness refuses to answer."

The counterman in the decrepit bistro did a double take when he saw Jim and Pat walk in at lunchtime. He showed them to a table without a word and dropped menus on the table as if they were toxic.

Jim pulled out a chair and sat down. "He's certainly glad to see us."

Pat studied the menu. "I'm here under duress. What do you hope will happen? Anders will burst from the kitchen saying, 'I confess!'"

"A war of attrition, my dear."

"We'll eat every meal here for the rest of our stay?"

Jim smiled. "Wait and see."

"Do I have a choice? If I want to be with you, that is, which at the moment is a dubious proposition."

Lunch was barely edible. Dinner was better. The house red was drinkable, Pat's cod enjoyable, and Jim's roast chicken good. They had asked for the check when Anders strolled out of the kitchen and, without preliminaries, sat down next to Jim. "Enough. What do I have to do to get you two to leave me alone?"

A softball question to start. "Clarify a few things for me. Max Ryan told me you had nothing to do with the Meyer lemon semifreddo the night Michael Spinner died. Is that correct?"

"Absolutely. Max and only Max prepared the semifreddo for Mr. Spinner whenever he ate with us."

"And something happened that night that hadn't happened before, according to Max."

"Yes, Teddy Demarco asked Max to personally carry the semifreddo to Mr. Spinner."

"And to your knowledge, that was unusual?"

"Never happened before, and I knew everything that happened in that kitchen. The kitchen was my domain. Satisfied?"

"Not yet. Did you notice any change in Max after he took the dessert to Spinner?"

"He seemed unusually emotional. I asked him if he was okay, and he told me Spinner had thanked him for preparing his favorite dessert every time he came in. Max had tears in his eyes when he told me. The emotion seemed unwarranted. I didn't know what to make of it."

"Had Max ever threatened Spinner, expressed hatred of him?"

Anders shrugged. "Everyone hated Spinner. He made nice with Teddy Demarco because Teddy owned the place and me because he liked my cooking, but he treated everyone else like dirt."

"But you called the DA after Spinner died and implicated Max. You didn't leave your name but it was you, wasn't it?"

Olaf Anders's stone face showed a crack or two. "How did you know about that? Okay, at the time I did think it was Max, but now I'm not so sure. Teddy Demarco wanted to buy Fish and Fowl from the landlord and had obtained Spinner's financial backing. Demarco was furious when Spinner failed to come through with the money."

"So you now think Teddy Demarco killed Spinner?"

"I no longer know what to think."

A lone customer entered the bistro and took a seat at the counter.

"I have to get back to the kitchen," Anders said. "You've come a long way for nothing."

"One final question. Did you tip off the DA to get rid of Max Ryan so he wouldn't reveal you were a drug addict, or if he did would just seem like a disgruntled former employee?"

Anders's pale skin reddened. "You have no right to ask that. I'm not on trial."

"I don't give a damn whether I have the right. A possibly innocent man has been in prison for twenty years."

Anders sneered, "And I'm cooking in this hell hole. Safe journey home to both of you," and stomped away.

"We're staying at the Hotel Figaro if you change your mind," Jim called.

Jim and Pat walked to the river. Jim spoke first. "I know, I know. Don't rub it in."

"I know what you were trying to do, but it didn't work."

"No kidding? I have no idea who killed Spinner, but I only have to decide whether I'm going to support Max's parole, not prove who did it."

They reached the river. A barge heading upstream swerved off course in the current and at the last minute deftly ducked under a bridge.

"Want to head home?" Jim asked.

"Let's wait a day or two," Pat said. "I've got a feeling Olaf Anders may have more to tell you."

"I thought you just said I blew it."

"I changed my mind."

"A foolish consistency is the hobgoblin of little minds."

"Jim, if the parole hearing were tomorrow, what would you do?"

"Nothing. It would break my heart, but at the moment my only reason for supporting Max Ryan is gut feeling. I need stronger reason than that."

The next day they wandered the small streets of their neighborhood, drank more wine than they should, and tried to enjoy Paris without thoughts of Max Ryan in a prison cell. The second day Olaf Anders called the hotel and asked to meet.

They met on the trailing end of Blvd St. Germain, away from tourists. Dressed in street clothes, Olaf looked more respectable.

He leaned his elbows on a small, round table and spoke without looking up. "I've been thinking. I didn't kill Michael Spinner but I may have contributed to his death."

"Explain."

"I put pressure on Spinner when he said he was backing out of the deal. I told him if he didn't help Teddy and me buy the restaurant, I would reveal to the world that he was a fraud and his hedge fund was going broke." Anders lifted his elbows from the table. "Try to understand, Spinner had *promised* us. He told Teddy and me he loved the restaurant and wanted to help us buy it so it would remain as is and he could keep eating there. Being head chef at my own restaurant had always my dream, and when he told us he didn't have the money, I lost it. I don't remember exactly what I said, but Spinner looked very rattled afterward."

Jim waited. Anders seemed relieved to have spoken.

"Did you ever tell the police what you just told me?" Jim said.

Anders shook his head. "No, how could I? I had successfully diverted suspicion toward Max. How could I admit I had lied?" He slumped in his chair.

"One more question. Spinner told you his hedge fund was belly-up?"

"He said he could stay afloat as long as new money kept coming in, but he didn't have the money to pay investors who wanted out."

"So it was a Ponzi-scheme all along?"

"It started out legit, but he got greedy and used investors' money to finance his newly extravagant lifestyle. Big mistake, he told me, and he begged me not to expose him. He loved Pamela Martin and didn't want her to know what bad shape he was in. She was the only good thing left in his life, he told me." Olaf looked out the window of the small café. "Spinner was a hard man with a soft center. I've spent twenty years wondering if I pushed him over the edge."

"Are you suggesting he killed himself?"

Anders nodded. "I think it's possible."

As Jim and Pat walked back to their hotel soon after, Jim asked her, "What do you think?"

"So Michael Spinner is profligate with other peoples' money until he meets Pamela Martin, reforms too late, goes bankrupt, and kills himself? I don't buy it. I think it's more likely that a man like Spinner would murder anyone who threatened to expose him, not kill himself."

Jim disagreed, "I buy suicide. I don't think that Spinner could stand the humiliation of being exposed as a fraud. I'll raise the possibility with Ted Conover when we're home."

"Are we going home?"

"I'm ready."
"Let's go."

12

Comfortable Cambridge with Harvard, MIT, Beauty Shop Row, and The Long Gone, seemed blah after Paris. But what could you do? He was thoroughly American and too old to move. And he loved the English language. He didn't know how much until he was surrounded by it again and could understand everything he heard and read.

His first stop after conceding a day to jet lag was Ted Conover's office.

"Where's your beret?" Ted asked.

"No beret, just new information."

"Tell me." Ted looked comfortable behind his desk.

"I located Olaf Anders, the chef at the Fish and Fowl the night Michael Spinner died. He's cooking at a crummy bistro in the 7th and is or was a cocaine addict. I got him to admit he threatened Spinner for reneging on a promise to fund the purchase of the Fish and Fowl."

"Physically threatened?"

"Threatened to expose his business failures. The detail that triggered my imagination was that Spinner was terrified his fiancée would find out he had gone broke. Are you with me so far?"

"Go on."

"Did your office consider the possibility that Spinner wasn't murdered, that he committed suicide?"

Ted linked his fingers under his chin. "I don't know. I was brand new in the DA's office and very junior at the time of Max Ryan's indictment."

Jim stirred in his seat. "What has bothered me from the start about the case is lack of motive. I'm even more puzzled with the passage of time. No offense, but Michael Spinner's death wouldn't be the first time the DA's office prematurely brought an indictment in a high-profile case. I understand the pressures that can be put on a DA. Michael Spinner had friends in high places and a high profile in the press. In some ways, Max Ryan didn't stand a chance."

Ted lowered his hands and leaned forward. "What do you want me to do?"

"Review the forensics. Arsenic killed Michael Spinner and was found on Max Ryan's clothes. Was it found anywhere else?"

"I know it wasn't found in food, because any food Ryan didn't finish was disposed of, but I'll go back and check the records with suicide in mind."

"Thank you." Jim started to rise.

"Is this your last shot, Jim? Have you run out of leads?"

"I'm afraid so."

"If this doesn't pan out, you won't support Ryan's parole?"

"Unless I come up with something else."

"I like you, as you know, and admire your impulse to right wrongs, but in truth, I hope you fail in this case. I have a vested interest in not showing up my predecessors. You understand."

Jim rose all the way. "Of course. I was part of the judicial system. It gets things right most of the time."

Ted stood. "It does, but once in a while, it screws up. I shall look at the record again and see what I can find." He reached across the desk and shook Jim's hand.

*

Jim walked to The Long Gone deep in thought. He stopped a block away and called Pamela Martin. She wasn't in, but he left a message.

Coffee was just what he needed. The Long Gone was half full. The hum of ear buds, the hiss of steam, gladdened his heart.

He thought back to Max Ryan's trial. He remembered his nerves more than the evidence. His first murder trial, a big deal, and his nerves were on edge. The only time he could remember being more nervous was when he put on his robe for the very first time. That time, he, Jim Randall, scared to death, was to hear a case of breaking and entering. He, Jim Randall, devoid of wisdom, was going to pretend he was wise. He, Jim Randall, was about to be exposed as a fraud, but it didn't happen, and gradually Jim grew confident in his role and became respected as a judge, though was known to be too full of himself now and then. But now, with his questions about Max Ryan's guilt, his confidence was coming full circle back to his time of self-doubt and nerves.

His phone interrupted his train of thought.

"Judge Randall, Pamela Martin. You called?"

"Yes. Just a minute. Let me go outside." He stood, his legs stiff after the long walk and short rest, and made his way to the sidewalk. "Okay, I can talk now. Thanks for returning my call."

"Have you uncovered new evidence?"

"Not quite. New doubts, which I would like to talk to you about. Can we meet?"

They arranged to meet the next morning at The Long Gone.

He stayed with Pat on Beacon Hill that night and told her about his day. "I sat at The Long Gone remembering my first trial. Breaking and entering. What was your first?"

Pat thought for a moment. "Domestic assault. Very sad case. I wanted to throw my gavel at the louse of a husband."

"It must have been hard as a new judge to keep your emotions in check."

Pat nodded. "I got better at it."

"Me too, but now I've come full circle and wonder, was I ever a good judge?"

"Was I? None of us can know for sure."

"I guess the only objective measurement is cases overturned on appeal, but that presupposes wise appellate judges."

"We do our jobs in hopes we are not as bad as we secretly fear," Pat said.

"Amen."

*

Pamela Martin arrived on time at The Long Gone, looking worried rather than eager. She nodded to Jim and pulled up a chair.

"You have me worried," she said.

"I don't mean to. Let me fill you in on what's happened since I last saw you. Pat and I went to Paris where I tracked down and met with Olaf Anders."

"He was the chef at the Fish and Fowl, wasn't he?"

"That's correct. He put a doubt in my mind that I wanted to share with you and get your reaction. It may be hard to hear." Jim gave her time to prepare. He had respect for Pamela Martin and hated to reopen old wounds, but Max Ryan was in prison. "Olaf Anders thinks your former fiancé may have committed suicide."

Pamela Martin recoiled. "Suicide?"

"I'm sorry."

"Why would he do that? We were happy."

"I believe you. From what I have learned, he loved you and shielded you from his financial troubles."

"I knew he was going through a difficult period."

"But you didn't know his world was teetering."

She put her palms on the table as if to bolt. "That's crazy. Michael was going through a rough patch but he would have recovered."

"I'm just telling you what I have found."

"Michael bragged about his wealth whenever I raised the age gap between us. He said his age and experience were advantages because they had helped him get rich. I didn't care about money, and I told him so, but he had bragging in his veins."

"The foundation he established in his will, did it ever get off the ground?"

"No. I think I told you this before. He died before he signed all the papers."

"And the will left nothing to you, correct?"

"Yes, and I didn't expect anything. Judge Randall, it may be hard for you to understand, but I never looked at Michael and saw money. I saw a charming, challenging man who was very much in love with me. Tell me, have you learned anything about Michael that would change my opinion of him? Because he was a good man, in spite of the things written about him. In fact, I stopped reading what was written about him long ago."

"I'm not trying to change your opinion of him, but Max Ryan is alive and in prison, and he's my concern now. If you think of anything else, no matter how small, any half-buried memory, will you please let me know?"

She looked pained. "I have a good life, Judge Randall. A husband I love, a daughter in high school, and a son in junior high. Please understand."

"I certainly do, and you've been very helpful to me. I only ask you to keep Max Ryan in mind for a while longer."

He heard back from Ted three days later.

"The forensics look solid, even after twenty years. Arsenic found on Max Ryan's clothes in sufficient amount for there to be no doubt what it was."

"Was arsenic found elsewhere in the kitchen?"

"No," Ted said.

"That's what I remembered from the trial. How about the dining room? Were any traces found in the dining room?"

"None. That doesn't mean much, though, since all the linen and tableware was washed each night."

"Was Michael Spinner's home tested?"

"No. He fell sick in the cab and was taken to the hospital. No reason to test his home."

"If his death was murder."

"Which was the assumption at the time of the investigation. Suicide wasn't considered since arsenic was found on Max Ryan."

"That doesn't mean it wasn't suicide."

"Arsenic is fast acting. Conceivably Spinner could have ingested the arsenic before he got to the restaurant, but then he would have had convulsions during dinner. No, Jim, it wasn't suicide."

"Have you learned anything new about Spinner's financial status at the time of death?"

"Nothing that helps. Spinner was adept at concealing his hedge funds from close scrutiny – he knew how to satisfy regulators without revealing much, not all that hard to do when you are essentially a one-man operation. Public records confirm his funds had done poorly leading up to his death, but nothing indicates he was on the verge of bankruptcy."

Jim answered. "Let's assume for a moment he was. For a man whose reputation and ego depended on spectacular gains for a select few clients, exposure as a failure could be devastating."

"That's certainly a possibility."

"And he was engaged to Pamela Martin. Maybe he couldn't stand the thought of losing her if she found out he was almost broke."

Ted thought carefully before he answered. "That still doesn't explain away the arsenic found on Max Ryan or the timeline. And speaking of time, you don't have much. The parole hearing is next week."

When Jim left Ted's office, he walked the short distance to the Charles River to think. Only when he got to the river did he wonder whether he did so to be reminded of the Seine. Not much similarity, but flowing water was flowing water. He needed to make up his mind, but he didn't know what to do.

He turned away from the Boston skyline and walked along the Cambridge shore. He wished to hell he had been a better judge at the time of Max Ryan's trial. He wished he had known when to push through the fog of testimony, when to prod the attorneys to get to the point – eventually he became good at structuring and pacing a trial, but he stunk during Max Ryan's trial.

13

Jim sat at the desk in his third-floor study. Out the window he could see the peaked roofs of Cambridge triple-deckers and the tops of trees. From the air, he was surprised to see how many trees there were in his neighborhood; from the street, the wood frame triple-decker houses predominated.

A trial had a pace, a rhythm, a beginning and an end. A judge could not refuse to decide, could not plead the equivalent of a hung jury, but Jim was no longer a judge and he was stuck.

When unsure what to do, move from your desk to your recliner and recline, preferably with your hands behind your head. Stare at the ceiling, find no inspiration there, and return to your desk. If luck is with you, a witness will call at that very moment with new information that will unlock the case.

Had he somehow tapped into the zeitgeist? Had his silent musings reached the master manipulator? His phone rang as he sat down at his desk.

"Hello?"

"Judge Randall?" A woman's voice.

"Yes. Who is this?"

"Pamela Martin. I thought of something else. It may be of no significance, but you said to tell you anything that came to my mind."

"I'm listening."

"I don't want to do this on the phone. Can we meet? I can come to the coffee house you like."

"The Long Gone. Yes. Tell me when."

"We need to do this soon. How about five o'clock today."

"I'll be there."

The end-of-work crowd packed The Long Gone. Jim took a rear table near the restroom in spite of the occasional whiff of urine that drifted under the door. The table was rarely occupied for that very reason, and at this hour was the only table where he and Pamela Martin could have some privacy, assuming the people doing their business behind the door didn't listen.

She looked preoccupied when she entered the coffee shop. When she didn't immediately spot Jim, she frowned. He stood up and waved to get her attention, and she joined him in the rear.

"I didn't see you," she said, sitting.

"How are you?"

"I remembered something Michael did the night he died. It didn't occur to me before now because it seemed so routine."

"Yes?"

"Michael excused himself to use the restroom before dessert. When he returned to the table, he seemed emotional."

"How so?"

"I attributed it to what he did next, ask to speak to Max Ryan. Michael could be a hard man at times but he could get emotional about small things like Meyer lemon semifreddo."

"Okay. Can you describe his emotion?"

"Sentimental. Sad. Nothing dramatic, I barely noticed it at the time, but he grew more emotional as the evening ended, and when we got in the cab, I thought he was going to cry."

"And that's when he took ill."

"In the cab, yes. I immediately knew something was wrong and asked to be taken to the hospital."

"Thank you. This is very helpful."

"Really?"

"Really."

For once, he didn't walk the long way home. Avoiding Beauty Shop Row and the live chickens, he walked directly to his townhouse and climbed to his study.

"Is he there?" Jim asked when Ted Conover's office answered the phone. "Judge Randall calling."

He was connected quickly.

"Yes, Jim."

"I may have found the answer."

"To what question?"

"How arsenic got on Max Ryan's clothes."

"I'm listening."

"Not yet. I have some follow-up to do first, but what I've learned makes me more inclined to think that Michael Spinner committed suicide."

"Interesting. You don't have much time to prove it."

"I know."

"What next?"

"I visit Max Ryan."

*

When Jim entered the prison, he thought how strange that Ryan would be up for parole in a very few days; he seemed a permanent part of the prison. It was hard to imagine him outside.

"Good news?" Ryan said when he entered the visitors room.

"I may have found something."

"Tell me."

Why had Jim not noticed the stained and cracked concrete before? Because when you're in a room like this, it pays to notice as little as possible, lest the room become real.

"Michael Spinner summoned you from the kitchen to thank you on the night of his death. Go over that again. Describe in detail what happened."

"I already did."

"Tell me again. Think hard. Exactly what did Spinner do?"

Max Ryan hesitated. "He grabbed my hand and shook it hard for a long time. He wouldn't let go."

"Think carefully. Did he touch any part of you other than your hand?"

"My arm."

"Describe."

"He gripped my bicep as he shook my hand."

"Which arm did he grip?"

"My right arm."

"Did he touch you anywhere else?"

"He hugged me after he shook my hand. What I remember most is how emotional he seemed. He had tears in his eyes. I couldn't figure out why since all he was doing was thanking me for the semifreddos. It was a little unnerving."

"Thank you. This is what I wanted to hear."

"I don't understand."

Jim signaled to the guard that he was ready to leave. "I don't think Michael Spinner was murdered. I think he committed suicide."

Jim didn't wait until he got home to call Ted Conover. He called from the prison parking lot before he got in his car. He couldn't reach him but left a message.

"Ted, it's Jim Randall. Can you please check the forensic report on the Ryan case again? Where exactly on Max Ryan's clothes were the traces of arsenic found? Thanks."

Jim ate dinner at Pat's that evening. He fidgeted while he ate. "What's keeping Ted?"

"He'll get back to you as soon as he has an answer, you know that," Pat said.

"He may drag his heels. He does represent the Commonwealth, you know." Jim shifted in his chair.

"Will you support Max Ryan if the forensic report doesn't confirm your theory?"

"I don't know. I want to."

"Were you always certain as a judge when you pronounced sentence?"

"Of course not. Neither were you, but we had to decide."

"Exactly my point, Jim. You made decisions when you had to, so did I. Ted will call back and you will do what you think is right, of those things I am certain. Everything else remains unclear."

Ted's call came the next morning. "You asked where on Max Ryan's clothes arsenic was found?"

"Yes."

"On the front of his shirt and the bicep of his right sleeve."

"Wonderful. That's what I wanted to hear."

14

Max Ryan's parole hearing was held in a prison conference room down the hall from the visiting room. Bigger room, same bleak feeling. A long table held all seven parole board members, looking alert and ready. Waiting in the back of the room to testify were Deborah Ryan, Pamela Martin, an assistant prison warden, the prison librarian, and Jim. Max Ryan sat by himself facing the parole board.

The chair of the board was an avuncular white-haired gentleman named Collins. When everyone was seated, he began, "The purpose of today's hearing is to consider the parole request of Max Ryan, who has served twenty-one years of his twenty-five to life sentence. The facts of his conviction, briefly stated are as follows...." Collins then recited the known facts of the case. When he finished, he addressed Max Ryan.

"Mr. Ryan, do you still maintain your innocence?"

"Yes, sir," Max said.

"You realize that if you expressed remorse, it would count in your favor in our decision."

"I realize that, but I can't express remorse for something I didn't do."

"Very well. We will proceed. To begin, please tell us in your own words how you have used your time in prison. I should state for the record that Mr. Ryan has no blemishes on his record." He gestured in Max Ryan's direction. "Go ahead, please. What have you done in prison to make productive use of your time?"

Max Ryan cleared his throat. He leaned forward, his expression simultaneously grim, determined, and childlike. Jim had never seen him look so focused, and it made him realize he didn't really know Max Ryan.

"Thank you. I will do my best. I have spent my time in prison trying to blend in, so it's going to be hard to stand out now. But I'll try." He leaned partway back in his chair. "I've spent most of my time since I've been here working in the kitchen. If I get out while I'm still young enough to work, I want to go back to cooking, so I've learned new skills while I've been here. It hasn't been easy, because the kitchen here is not well equipped, but I've managed.

"When I'm not in the kitchen, I've read. I've read more than ever in my life. I figured I couldn't stay the way I was, as soon I got in prison I realized that. I had to either improve or decline, I couldn't stay the same. So I read. I read philosophy, especially the Stoics, and religion – I am drawn to Buddhism and the idea that this is just a passage. Some things make me too sad. Fiction, for example, makes me realize what I'm missing by being on the inside. And I read some politics. I can't believe what some of our leaders are doing. Why aren't *they* in prison?"

Three of the parole board members smiled, then Chairman Collins asked a follow-up. "Mr. Ryan, you do not sound angry even after spending twenty years in prison for something you say you didn't do. Are you an excellent actor, or have you managed to avoid hating the people who put you here?"

"I was angry at first. Very angry. I couldn't believe it. What was I doing here? I hardly knew Michael Spinner. I made desserts for him, and for that I wound up in jail? I was furious. But I came to realize that anger would destroy me, and reading Buddhism helped me maintain perspective. What happened to me was wrong, but injustices happen all the time to many people, and I just happened to be one of the unlucky ones."

"Do you have a support system outside if you are released?"

"My wife, Deborah, who is in the room, has stood with me all this time. Without her, all the reading in the world wouldn't have helped me avoid hating the people who put me here."

"You will have an opportunity to say more after we hear from several people who want to testify on your behalf, but for now I'd like to hear from the assistant warden and the librarian."

The assistant warden was youngish, roughhewn, and spoke with a heavy Boston accent. After preliminaries, he lauded Max Ryan's efforts in the kitchen. "Mr. Ryan essentially runs the kitchen. When I became assistant warden six years ago and ate in the cafeteria for the first time, I couldn't believe how good the food was, and Max Ryan did it without high-tech equipment or premium quality ingredients. I don't have an opinion on his guilt or innocence, but he is a hell of a cook."

The librarian, a woman in her fifties, said similar things. "Max Ryan is a serious student, an avid reader. I've had to borrow books from other prison libraries to meet his requests."

Next came Max Ryan's loyal wife, Deborah.

When she first introduced herself to Jim at The Long Gone, she had looked long-suffering, now she looked hopeful. But her manner was subdued, respectful. "Max is a good man," she began. "If he wasn't I wouldn't stick with him."

"How did you two meet?" Collins asked.

"We grew up on the same block. I was two years older than Max, so we didn't run with the same crowd, but you can't help but know everybody on the block. What I noticed about Max is he seemed old for his age. He mostly stayed out of trouble because he was able to tell the bullies no. I noticed that. Tough guys run in packs, they're scared to do things on their own. Max knew what he wanted and went for it."

"What did he want?"

"To be a chef. He cooked for me and my sister one time. He made spaghetti carbonara and it was the best thing I had ever eaten. He was, like, fifteen. I don't know where he got the talent because his mother couldn't cook and his father had passed. His mother's cooking was so bad my mother used to make jokes about it. They were friends so she was entitled to. Max had a quiet soul, even then, and since he's been in prison he has grown so much. I can't wait until he gets out. It will be so nice to have him home."

Other board members asked her questions, and then Jim strode to the front of the room. Chairman Collins started by saying, "It is highly unusual for a judge who put a man in prison to appear at his parole hearing. In fact, in my memory, it has never happened before. Welcome, Judge Randall. Glad to have you here."

"Glad to be here," Jim replied, pulling up his chair to the table.

"May I ask, what made you decide to come today?"

Jim scanned the parole board members, sensed Max Ryan seated next to him, was aware of Deborah Ryan and Pamela Martin sitting behind him. He felt awkward and out of place and tried to imagine himself on his bench in his judicial robe rather than wearing street clothes at a parole hearing in a prison conference room.

"I usually find it hard to recreate reasons for doing something, but in this case my curiosity was triggered by Mrs. Ryan introducing herself to me at a coffee shop I frequent and telling me her husband was up for parole. Max Ryan's case was my first murder trial as a judge, so I remembered it well. Partly to see how I did as a young judge, partly because something about Deborah Ryan's concern for her husband touched me, I decided to review his case. She did not exaggerate, she did not plead, she did not beg."

"Very well," Chairman Collins said. "Continue."

"You have heard glowing words about Max Ryan and how he has used his time in prison. I am here today to talk about something more fundamental, his guilt or innocence of the crime for which he was convicted. My investigation has convinced me there is substantial doubt of his guilt, and believe me, I understand the implications of that statement. If I am correct now, I was wrong when I sentenced him. Hard to admit, but true."

He paused. He had the panel's full attention.

"I have found substantial reasons to believe that Michael Spinner was not murdered, that he committed suicide. Keep in mind that the only forensic evidence was arsenic traces found on the clothes Max Ryan wore in the kitchen, but I discovered an alternative explanation for how the arsenic got there. Before I get to that, a little background. Michael Spinner was in deep financial trouble at the time of his death, trouble that he was trying to keep secret. His hedge fund had lost so many investors it was virtually broke. He couldn't pay his investors who wanted to cash out, couldn't keep the financial commitments he made, and was terrified that his fiancé would leave him if she found out he was broke. He was a man whose ego hinged on his reputation, and when he feared exposure as a failure, he crumbled. In my experience, men like Michael Spinner do not have emotional reserves to fall back on, they fly high or they crash. Keep a few key facts in mind – arsenic is a fast-acting poison. Michael Spinner was fine when he picked Pamela Martin up in a taxi to go to dinner. Their dinner was leisurely, lasting almost two hours. Michael Spinner fell violently ill in the taxi going home after dinner. Therefore he was poisoned *during* dinner, not before. The question is, who poisoned him? According to is Ms. Martin, Michael Spinner was unusually sentimental the night he died. After listening to her, I think you will have reasonable doubt as to whether a murder took place that night. With your permission, I'll ask Pamela Martin to step forward."

"You may proceed."

Jim turned and nodded to Pamela. She came forward and sat beside Jim. She clenched her hands tightly together.

Chairman Collins said, "Welcome. Please introduce yourself to the panel."

Pamela slid her chair close to the table. "My name is Pamela Martin. I was engaged to be married to Michael Spinner and was with him the night he died."

"Please tell us in your own words what he did and said that night."

"Two things stick in my mind, even after twenty intervening years. The first was how emotional Michael was. He was a tightly controlled man, especially in public, yet he came close to tears when he told me how much I meant to him. He told me as if he knew he wouldn't see me again, and, as it turned out, he wouldn't. I think of it now and wonder why I didn't realize something was terribly wrong. The second thing that sticks in my mind is something Michael did that differed from all the other times we ate at the Fish and Fowl. He asked the restaurant owner to have Max Ryan come from the kitchen so Michael could personally thank him for preparing his favorite dessert whenever we ate there. Mr. Ryan was the assistant pastry chef and always had Meyer lemon semifreddo ready for Michael. Michael *loved* Mr. Ryan's semifreddo. When Mr. Ryan emerged from the kitchen, Michael hugged him and emotionally shook his hand. Even then I thought it was over the top, and in retrospect, it reinforces my impression that Michael knew he was approaching the end of his life and was tying up loose ends."

She seemed startled by how forcefully she had expressed her opinion. She paused, which let Jim ask a question. "You told me something else your fiancé did that night, something he did before he asked to see Max Ryan."

She nodded. "Yes."

"Would you tell the panel?"

"Michael excused himself from the table to use the restroom. He was away from the table a long time, and when he came back, that's when he teared up and told me how much I meant to him. That's when he asked to speak to Max Ryan."

Chairman Collins looked at his fellow panel members, then at Pamela Martin. "You have heard Judge Randall state his opinion that your fiancé committed suicide. Do you share that opinion?"

"Yes. It was hard for me to accept, but I now think that Michael swallowed the arsenic when he went into the restroom, which could explain his emotional state afterward. He knew what was about to happen, what did happen. Michael fell violently ill in the cab home and died in the hospital that night."

Chairman Collins said, "Judge Randall, I ask you as an experienced jurist, how do you explain the arsenic found on Max Ryan's clothing?"

"The handshake and hug. If Michael Spinner ingested the arsenic when he went to the restroom, some may have spilled on his hand and clothes. Imagine: he was committing suicide, his hands undoubtedly were shaking, and when he thanked Max Ryan, some of the arsenic got on Ryan. May I demonstrate?"

"Go ahead."

Jim and Pamela stood. He gave her a hug, then grasped her biceps with one hand and shook her hand with the other. As he did, he continued talking. "I can't prove this is how it happened, but I don't need to. This is a parole hearing, not a trial. If there is substantial doubt a murder was committed that night, then surely Max Ryan should be paroled. He may have served twenty-one years in prison for a suicide."

Chairman Collins glanced at the other panel members. "Thank you, Judge Randall. Do the panel members have any other questions of these two witnesses?" There were none. Chairman Collins then addressed Pamela Martin. "Thank you, Ms. Martin. You didn't have to come today. It was a brave act. The panel and I thank you. And thank you, Judge Randall. I can't recall another instance where a judge supported the parole of a man he sentenced. It speaks highly of you."

Jim shook his head. "I had to. Max Ryan should not be in prison."

There was more testimony, including confirmation from Max Ryan that events had been as Pamela Martin described, but everything after her testimony and Jim's seemed anticlimactic.

"We will issue our decision in due time," Chairman Collins concluded. "This panel is adjourned."

*

At Pat's that night, Jim had a minor meltdown. He hadn't realized how tense he had been these past weeks.

Jim's minor meltdowns were barely noticeable to someone who didn't know him well. Pat knew him well and gave him enough space to breathe, to expand his lungs to full capacity, to unkink the muscles of his neck, but stayed close enough to prop him up when he sagged.

"I stunk today. Thank God it doesn't all depend on me."

"You did fine. What do you think the decision will be?"

"The other witnesses were great. Especially Pamela Martin, bless her heart. It must have been a struggle for her to decide to testify and to do it without anger. I do not understand that kind of forgiveness."

They were sitting in Pat's comfortable, well-appointed living room looking across a narrow, precipitous street at the brightly lit windows of Beacon Hill.

"I have to snap out of this," he said. "I did the best I could. His fate is not in my hands."

"To play the devil's advocate for a minute..."

"Do you have to?"

"No, but I'm going to. Worse comes to worse, Max Ryan serves four more years and then is released."

"Easy for you to say."

Pat stood and came to the chair where Jim was sitting. It had become his de facto chair whenever he stayed over. She nudged him to one side. "Move over."

Jim protested. "There isn't room for both of us in this chair. What are you doing?"

"Pretending that we like each other. Move over."

He did as he was told. She half-sat in the chair, half-sat on him.

"I can barely breathe," he feigned.

"That is my purpose."

"Affixation?"

"They say it improves sex."

"You have a filthy mind, Your Honor."

"So do you."

"I'll see you in your chambers. Now."

15

Sasha Cohen of the Boston *Globe* called the next day. "A source told me that you appeared before the parole board yesterday."

"Yes, I did."

"So it's true? You supported the parole of a man you sentenced?"

"I did what I thought appropriate."

"That's impressive, Jim. Not many judges would do that."

"I don't find it so unusual. I tried to do the right thing during the trial and I tried to do the right thing now."

"You're a mensch. When the parole board's decision is made public, will you give me an exclusive?"

"No, but I'll treat you to lunch."

It could be weeks before the board made its decision, depending on the board's case load. Jim second-guessed himself for days after the hearing. What could I have done better? Did I do the right thing? He consoled himself with reminders that even without his support, Max Ryan had a fair chance of parole because of his clean record in prison and the testimony of the librarian and the head of the kitchen. It doesn't all depend on me, Jim mused. He had gotten into the habit when a judge of having the last word, of being the final arbitrator. Having so much power made him uncomfortable at times but came to be something he missed when he stepped down from the bench. Important for him to remember that he was a bit player in the parole board's decision.

Yes, but the fact that he was the judge who sent Ryan to prison undoubtedly carried weight.

He occupied himself by going through his papers in his study. He had three wooden file cabinets full of his personal papers and being a packrat he rarely threw anything out. Pat, on the other hand, only kept what was necessary for personal reasons or archival purposes. The difference in the quantity and organization of his papers was one reason Jim got bogged down when writing their memoir. Or so he consoled himself.

Some of what he found in his file cabinets appalled him – law school stuff, high school stuff. Had he been as dumb as all that? Yet he had become a judge. A good judge, he believed. Had he overestimated himself as a judge? He didn't believe he was any dumber or less prepared than the average judge. So the justice system depends on a host of not-so-dumb, not-so-smart judges? Scary. The saving grace being "the system." Nothing depended entirely on one person – there were dueling attorneys, there were juries, there was the possibility of appeal. The system. All hail the system, the oh-so-fallible but nonetheless precious system of justice.

Add parole boards to that inventory, parole boards that can mitigate the mistakes of novice judges.

He and Pat ate at Duck, Duck, Goose three times before the parole board issued its decision. Bruce gave them their usual corner table by the window.

Jim couldn't help quipping when he scanned the dessert menu the first evening, "What, no Meyer lemon semifreddo?" The waiter answered solemnly, "No, sir, I'm afraid not," not noticing Jim's tongue in cheek.

Pat ordered chocolate mousse while Jim skipped dessert. "I wonder what will become of Max Ryan if he is granted parole," Jim wondered. "He and his wife seem devoted to each other, so that's a plus, but I worry he won't be able to find a job. Ex-cons have a hard time getting work."

"Jim, you can only do so much. Stop torturing yourself."

"I am doing no such thing."

Bruce came to the table. "How was dinner?"

"Wonderful," Pat said.

"Not your worst," Jim groused.

Fortunately Bruce knew Jim well. "Please don't repeat that on Yelp."

"What the hell is Yelp?"

"Hang on." Bruce disappeared in back, and a few moments later, a waiter brought two small glasses of pale liquid to the table.

"What's this?" Jim said, "We didn't order anything."

"Compliments of the house," the waiter explained. "Bruce thought you could use a treat."

*

Young people like Ernie Farrell gave Jim hope. Jim had successfully represented Ernie in court after his retirement, and they had remained friends since. He texted Ernie and suggested meeting at The Long Gone. When Ernie walked into the coffee shop, his hair was combed and his clothes were neat. He nodded at Jim, ordered coffee at the counter, and carried it to the table. "You look the same," he said, sitting down.

"You don't. You look dressed for an office."

"I work in an office."

"You call that an office?"

"You've only been there once."

"So?"

"Your powers of observation are good, but not that good."

Jim admitted defeat. "I'm waiting to hear what the parole board decides. No word yet."

"Any hints?"

"None."

"Are you working on any other cases?"

"No. I'll take a break after this. It's been nonstop since I retired."

Ernie scooted his chair back just enough to sit sidesaddle, legs crossed at the knee. "You know why I look different to you? I just realized. When I split from my ex-wife whose name shall not be uttered, I felt like a new person. I must have started dressing differently or something."

"You hate your ex so much you can't mention her name?"

Ernie uncrossed his legs. "I'm covering my shame with vitriol. The failure of my marriage was as much my fault as hers. Satisfied?"

"You've got nothing on me. I sent an innocent man to prison."

"A jury did."

"I presided. There were a million ways I could've changed the outcome. In a way, what's hardest is that admitting error makes me aware I probably made many mistakes equally as bad. Easier to close one's mind to the possibility, and I've known a lot of people who do, including me most of the time."

Ernie leaned back. "Tell me, Judge, who wins the prize for unwarranted certitude, the young or the old?"

"It's probably a draw. The young are certain out of insecurity, the old out of fear."

"Aren't they the same thing?"

"Related but not the same. The young feel nebulous in a world with defined edges. The old cling to their certainties in lieu of stopping time."

Ernie responded with silence at first. "I think I understand."

"Don't take me too seriously. When I finish a case I inevitably feel a letdown, and it leads to philosophizing. Keep me busy and I'm pleasantly superficial."

Pat stayed at Jim's townhouse that weekend. They bought a prepared chicken at the market around the corner, and Jim opened a bottle of Vacqueyras. Cambridge houses are jumbled together, unbroken straight lines being frowned on in an intellectual town, and Jim's rear neighbor was closer than his side neighbors. Lights were on in all the neighbor's rooms. Must be having a party. Or rebelling against energy efficiency.

Jim raised his glass. "To Max Ryan."

Pat followed suit. "And Deborah Ryan."

"And Pamela Martin for her courage and grace."

They clicked glasses and drank.

The parole board issued its decision on Monday.

Decision
In the matter of

Maxwell P. Ryan
W989735

Summary

This case presented unique issues for the board to consider. Normally the board considers such factors as the likelihood of recidivism, the conduct of the prisoner while incarcerated, the existence or non-existence of a support system upon release, etc. In this case, the board was presented with a much starker issue: a possible miscarriage of justice in the trial of the petitioner, Max Ryan, a possibility raised by none other than the presiding judge in the trial, retired judge James Randall, formerly of the Massachusetts Superior Court. The board can remember no similar case.

After considering all the testimony and the written record, the petitioner's request for parole is granted, with the following stipulations: one-to-one counseling upon release to assist in the transition; weekly visits to the Parole Office for a period of one year; GPS monitoring at the discretion of the parole officer. Violation of any of the terms of parole will result in revocation of parole.

The summary was followed by a lengthy recounting of the facts, the testimony, and the findings. The decision concluded by recommending referral of Max Ryan's case to the governor for possible exoneration.

Pat had gone back to Beacon Hill and called Jim immediately when she heard the news. "Congratulations. This may be the single best thing you have ever done."

"Better than being astounding in bed?"

"Close call, that."

"We were going to spend the night apart, but I want to be with you."

"Sounds like a good idea."

"Your place or mine?"

"You pick."

"Beacon Hill it is."

Next to call was Ted Conover. "I admire you, you old scoundrel."

"Even though I made your office look bad?"

"At least I wasn't the ADA who tried the case."

"Only because you were too green."

"Meet for a drink one of these days?"

"You name the day."

Then, Sasha Cohen, who asked, "Ready to give me the exclusive inside story?"

"No, but I'm ready to treat you to a latte at The Long Gone."

They arranged a time. Jim arrived first. Sasha waltzed in five minutes later and joined Jim at his table.

"You always get here before me. How do you do it?"

"By being an old person with nothing else to do."

Sasha sat down. "If you are old, I can't wait to be old."

"Don't say that. Old is the end stage, the final act."

"But you will get thunderous applause when you go."

"Maybe a tepid clap or two, that's all."

"Max Ryan will certainly join in."

"I have to tell you, Sasha, when I visited him in prison he struck me as a guy with nothing to hide, and my opinion never changed as I investigated. What a tragedy. Twenty-one years stolen from a man because we fallible humans didn't have the imagination to consider suicide as the cause of death."

"Jim, I agree with you but in a way it's no more tragic than a lightning strike or a tree falling on a passing car."

"Except that the tragedy was caused by people, not by a random act of nature. I'm sure there wasn't a single soul on that jury who didn't want to do the right thing. I sure as hell didn't want to screw up my first murder trial, and the DA didn't want to convict an innocent man, of that I'm sure. That is the tragedy. Good intentions all around, a justice system designed to avoid this kind of mistake, and still — and still — a colossal mistake. It makes me want to weep."

Max Ryan was released from prison a week later. According to his wife who was there to meet him, he emerged with the dazed look of a man whose brain could not process the enormous change that had just occurred. She drove him home, helped him into the house, and that was that. Incarcerated/free, in/out, flip a coin.

Deborah reported to Jim later that all her husband wanted to eat the first day was chocolate chip ice cream. He spent most of his time lying on the living room sofa watching talk shows with the sound turned down. Several of the first nights he awoke demanding to know what he was doing in a dark room he didn't recognize, then sobbing when he realized where he was. She wondered, she told Jim, if Max would ever again be the man she married. He had to tell her that, no, he would never be that man again, but he would recover.

Little by little Max gained the confidence to venture out of the house. He took walks around the neighborhood.

He accompanied Deborah to the grocery store (where the multiplicity of choices made him light-headed). Shopping malls seemed bigger, flashier, than he remembered, and he didn't recognize Boston's skyline. Deborah drove him by Fenway Park, which opened the floodgates of memory, and he regaled Deborah with stories of Yaz and Fisk the rest of the day, coming more to life with each story.

*

Three months after Max's release, Jim and Pat invited Max and Deborah Ryan to dinner at Duck, Duck, Goose. Jim was aware of the significance of the invitation: inviting a recently paroled, wrongly convicted pastry chef to a restaurant known for good food. Would it remind Max of all he had missed by having his dream of becoming a chef prematurely ended? Would it bring back dark memories of semifreddos and false accusations?

Max and Deborah arrived at the restaurant five minutes early. "Habit," Max explained. "Our privileges were docked if we were late to anything." He was wearing a bright red tie which clashed with his overall drab appearance − Jim couldn't help but think that prison had drained Max of color from the inside out, that he didn't look wan from lack of sun.

Bruce seated them at the corner table.

"This looks like a nice place," Max said, surveying the restaurant.

"Are you okay being here? It doesn't bring back painful memories of the Fish and Fowl?"

Max replied with an equanimity Jim envied, "Not going to dwell on that. I'm here to enjoy myself. This is our first good restaurant meal since my release." Max looked at Deborah and tried without much success to smile.

Deborah explained to Jim and Pat. "Max has been having nightmares. It's been hard for him."

"I can imagine," Jim said, then corrected himself. "Actually, I can't. If it happened to me, I think I'd want to take a gun and kill the people who did it to me."

"That's just the thing," Max said, "who would I shoot? Who were the bad guys?"

"Me. The system," Jim said.

"The system is bulletproof, and you redeemed yourself," Max replied. "I'm just grateful I'm out. I'll be fine. It'll take time, but I'll be fine."

Deborah spoke. "Judge Randall, I don't know how to thank you."

"There's no need to. If you hadn't spoken to me at The Long Gone I wouldn't have known Max was up for parole. Besides, as I told Max, he had a good chance of being released even without my involvement."

"Yes, but you brought so much weight to the hearing. I could tell by watching the faces of the parole board members."

"I'm going to order wine," Jim said. "Are you two wine drinkers?"

"Deborah definitely is," Max said. "I'm being cautious about alcohol since I got out."

"I think that's wise. I'll order some and keep close tabs on how much you drink." Jim's grin made Max smile for the first time. His smile was rusty.

They were silent while they looked at the menu.

Max looked up, chagrined. "I don't know what the hell half of this is. What is escabeche, and since when is kale the main ingredient of a salad?"

"Don't ask me," Jim said. "I know the difference between frozen and canned, as long as I can see the packaging. That's about it."

Pat advised, "Stick to food you know until you get used to what has changed."

Jim said, "That's good advice in general."

The waiter came and took their order. Max ordered beet salad and hangar steak, well done.

"Judge, what do you think my chances of exoneration are?"

"The political climate is hostile to anything that smacks of leniency, but I think you have a reasonable chance."

"No matter what, I'm grateful to you, very grateful."

Jim adopted his judicial mien. "No more thanks from you two or I'll hold you in contempt."

As they ate, Max fell into occasional silences. He would seem to be enjoying himself, then fall into a funk. Watching him, Deborah looked worried.

Pat broke the tension by saying, "How is your food?"

Deborah: "Fine." Max: "Tops the Fish and Fowl." He lowered his fork, came close to tearing up, then took another mouthful.

The wine pleased Jim, as did the dinner in general. When they were asked if they wanted to see a dessert menu, the answer was a unanimous yes, with Max's yes the most resounding.

When the menu came, his face creased in consternation. "'Dirty chai ice cream sandwich with rooibos crumble.' I have no idea what that is. That's what I'll have. This I have to see." He lowered the menu. "Do they ever serve Meyer lemon semifreddo here?"

"No, but maybe Bruce could use someone who's an expert."

"Who's Bruce?"

"Co-owner. I'll introduce you on the way out."

"No way he'll hire an ex-con."

"Have you started looking for work?"

"Not seriously. I've been freeloading on Deborah."

"It can't hurt to know Bruce."

Max dipped his head in thanks. "Once more, I owe you."

"I told you, no more thanks, and I meant it."

Jim made the introductions on their way out. The two couples stood on the sidewalk outside the restaurant.

"Live up to your parole requirements," Jim said.

"Don't worry."

"Because if you screw up, I'll come down on you very hard."

"I'm not going to screw up."

They looked each other in the eye and firmly shook hands.

"I'm not going to grip your arm. Don't worry."

Max and Deborah started to walk away.

"One more thing," Jim said.

Max turned. "Yes?"

"Did you do it?"

Max smiled, "Of course not." The smile was enigmatic and for a moment, Jim wondered if he had been played.

Deborah slapped Max's arm, "That's awful, Max. After all the judge did for you. Apologize."

"Just kiddin', Judge. Couldn't resist. Of course I didn't do it." Max waved over his shoulder as he and Deborah walked away.